"Even in the darkest moments of the story, hope tarries in the wings. A wonderful writer, a wonderful read."

Liz Curtis Higgs, New York Times bestselling author

"These tender and charming tales of medieval monastic life have an unexpectedly modern dimension. They highlight the struggles of the human condition both in the present and in the past. They illuminate that all humankind, whether aware of it or not, is on a pilgrimage. Through these stories we accompany Father Peregrine and his monks on their journey as they struggle to overcome their personal defects and to live harmoniously in community for the glory of God."

Eleanor Stewart, author, *Kicking the Habit*

"Poignant, moving, rich with imagery and emotion... Modern readers will easily identify with each character in Wilcock's timeless human dramas of people learning to love and serve one another while growing in their understanding of a tender and compassionate God. Highly recommended."

Midwest Book Review

"Wonderfully insightful, with a rich historical storyline. There's more substantial content here than in much Christian fiction – about grace, about leadership and loyalty, about humility, about disability and suffering."

FaithfulReader.com

The Wounds of God

PENELOPE WILCOCK

LION FICTION

Published by Lion Fiction
an imprint of
Lion Hudson plc
Wilkinson House, Jordan Hill Road
Oxford OX2 8DR, England
www.lionhudson.com/fiction

ISBN 978 1 78264 141 4
e-ISBN 978 1 78264 142 1

This edition 2015

A catalogue record for this book is available from the British Library

Printed and bound in the UK, January 2015, LH26

Contents

For my friend
Margery May

The Community of St Alcuin's Abbey

Monks

Brother Edward	*infirmarian*
Father Chad	*prior*
Father Columba	*abbot – known as Father Peregrine*
Brother John	*works in the infirmary*
Brother Gilbert	*precentor*
Brother Cyprian	*porter/infirmary patient*
Father Matthew	*novice master*
Brother Walafrid	*herbalist/winemaker*
Brother Giles	*assistant herbalist*
Brother Michael	*works in the infirmary*
Brother Andrew	*cook*
Brother Ambrose	*cellarer*
Brother Clement	*works in the scriptorium and library*
Brother Fidelis	*gardener, with special care of the roses*
Brother Peter	*cared for horses*
Brother Mark	*beekeeper*
Brother Stephen	*responsible for the farm*
Brother Martin	*porter*
Brother Paulinus	*gardener*
Brother Dominic	*guestmaster*
Brother Prudentius	*works on the farm*
Brother Basil	*elderly brother, assists in guest house*

Father Bernard	*cellarer in training*
Brother Germanus	*works on the farm*
Father Gerard	*almoner*

Novices and postulants

Brother Thomas	*abbot's esquire; also works on the farm*
Brother Francis	*works in a variety of locations*
Brother Theodore	*works mainly as a scribe and illuminator*
Brother Cormac	*works in the kitchen*
Brother Thaddeus	*works in a variety of locations*
Brother Richard	
Brother Damian	
Brother Josephus	
Allen Howick	*becomes Brother James*

Sick or aged brothers living in the infirmary

Brother Denis	*once the beekeeper*
Father Aelred	
Father Anselm	
Father Paul	
Father Gerald	
Father Lucanus	

Deceased community brethren mentioned in
The Hawk and the Dove

| Father Gregory | *previous abbot of the community* |

Assistants to the community

Martin Jonson	*lay worker in the infirmary*
Luke	*kitchen assistant*
Simon	*kitchen assistant*

CHAPTER ONE

About These Stories

I will never forget my friend Maggie dying. Word came to me on the Saturday afternoon that there had been a fire at her house and she was in hospital. I cancelled my plans for the evening and went straight there. I was not allowed to go in to her, the doctor was with her, so I sat down to wait in a room where chairs and bits of furniture were stored. Presently a plump, fair-haired, rather anxious-looking priest appeared in the corridor, looking for a nurse. He turned out to be Father Michael, one of the priests from the church Maggie attended. We sat in the small, cluttered room together, waiting, exchanging what news we had, what little we had heard, giving details to a nurse to fill in a form about Maggie; the sparse pitiful details of her lonely life.

Then we saw a nun walking briskly along the corridor, her veil flowing behind her. She marched straight up to the door of the intensive care unit. Maggie was there, and she intended to be with her. It was Sister Kathleen, the Irish nun, one of Maggie's friends from the convent. They wouldn't let her in, so all three of us sat together and waited, bound into a strange intimacy by the tension of the situation.

The doctor came to see us. She was very poorly, he said. She had seventy, maybe eighty, per cent burns. The right leg—most of the right side—was gone. He suggested we should not go and see her. The nurse agreed with him. It was not a pleasant sight, she said, even for a nurse. I felt glad enough to go along with the advice. What could we do, after all? She was unconscious. The priest, also with some relief, agreed with me. Sister Kathleen said nothing. The doctor went away, saying he would bring us more news later. Not until he had gone did Sister Kathleen speak: 'Should you not anoint her, Father?'

Of course. Of course he had to. We found the nurse again and explained. There were prayers that must be said: she must be anointed, blessed, absolved, before she died. Sister Kathleen said firmly that she would like to be there at Maggie's bedside to join in with the prayers. Me too. I knew it then. Just to creep away would not do. The nurse said she would go and ask. Where did Father want to anoint her? The forehead, he explained, was the usual place. The nurse looked doubtful. There's not much of her forehead left,' she said.

She went away and returned a moment later. Yes, there was a little place. It would be possible. The priest and I looked at each other. He did not speak, but there was a sort of barely perceptible wobbling about his face. I think he felt the same cold nausea of horror that I did. I don't know what Sister Kathleen was feeling. We trailed in the wake of her intrepid resolution, through the ward into the sideward where Maggie lay on her back under a sheet. Only her face was showing, and she was attached to all the tubes and drips of intensive care.

I don't know what I expected to see. I thought she would look like a piece of toast from what they said. It was Maggie, that's all. Maggie, with her face swollen and her hair singed, some of her skin burned away, the rest of it discoloured. But it was Maggie. I could see her soul. I don't mean my eyes saw a shining thing or anything like that. I mean that my spirit perceived, knew, beheld, the childlike, sweet reality of Maggie's real self, radiating from the still, burned body on the bed. Father Michael anointed her, and we said the prayers, and went home.

She was still alive in the morning. I was angry with myself for not having stayed with her. Maggie, who was so afraid of dying alone. I went back to the hospital and asked to sit with her.

'You can hold her hand,' said the nurse. 'Sit on this side. There's a bit more of this hand left.'

Again the cold, sick clutch of horror. What would it look like, the remains of that hand? The nurse lifted the sheet, and there it was, Maggie's hand. That's all it was; it was her hand. Burned, yes, and a lot of the skin gone, but it was Maggie's hand, and I held her hand till she died.

I have always been grateful for the clear-headed courage of that Irish nun, not discouraged by medical professionals or intimidated by unfamiliar territory and the instincts of fear and dread, remembering the human essentials. Maggie needed us; she needed us and she needed God, and in some strange way those needs were not separate but the same.

I walked away from the hospital down to the sea, wanting to be by myself, not ready to go home yet. I watched the waves crashing onto the pebbles as the tide came in, seeing and yet not seeing the foam and surge of the sea; half there and half still standing in the presence of death's mystery; fear, reverence, awe... My lips still remembered the cold, dead brow I had kissed in farewell. My eyes still saw the sharp outline of her face, no longer softened by colour or blurred by the constant undercurrent motion of breath, pulse, life. Once, just once, the fingers of her hand had moved while I held it, while the respirator still held together the last shreds of her life's breaking thread. Had she heard my voice? Talking so quietly, not wanting the nurse to hear: 'Forgive us, Maggie. Oh forgive us.' Maybe things would have turned out differently if I had stayed with her, been there to avert the last fatal stupidity: the spilt brandy, the dropped cigarette. I didn't know. I wished I still had my mother to talk it over with. Mother always understood my questions, spoken or unspoken, and my grieving—even this grief all numbed by regret. I remember how I used to come home to her with my troubles when I was a girl, and she always understood. I picture her now in the kitchen,

11

washing up maybe, or slicing potatoes, or stirring custard. She would listen quietly, and as often as not she would ponder my words for a few moments, then say, 'I know a story about that.' She would tell me stories, wonderful stories, that teased out the tangled threads of my heartaches and made sense of things again.

It was a monk Mother used to tell me stories about; a monk of the fourteenth century called Peregrine du Fayel. He was a badly disabled man with a scarred face and a lame leg and twisted, misshapen hands. He was the abbot of St Alcuin's Abbey in North Yorkshire, on the edge of the moors. He was a man whose body was shaped by the cruelties of life, but his spirit was shaped by the mercy and goodness of God. He couldn't do much with his broken hands, but he discovered that there were some precious and powerful things that could be done only by a man whom life had wounded badly. He was loved and honoured by the brothers who served God under him, and there were many stories told of his dealings with them, the things he said and did. These stories were never written in a book, but they have been passed down by the women in my family, from one generation to another.

The one who first collected the stories was a woman like him. In actual fact, although he kept this to himself, she was his daughter. Before he entered monastic life, he had a love affair, and unwittingly left his sweetheart expecting a baby. The baby, Melissa, was brought up by her mother and stepfather, and not until she was a young woman did she accidentally come across Abbot Peregrine, her real father. Finding him brought her a sense of completion and belonging, and she used to visit him in his monastery, and grew to love him very much, treasuring the stories about him that she gathered from the monks.

One of the stories they liked to tell her was the story of his name. His name in religion, the name his abbot had bestowed on him when he took his first vows and severed himself from all that he had been up until then, was 'Columba'. It is the Latin word

12

for a dove. The abbot had been named 'Peregrine' by his mother, because even as a baby it had been evident that he was going to inherit his father's proud, fierce, hawkish face—and he did. The brothers of Abbot Peregrine's monastery found the incongruity of the name 'Columba' very amusing. They called him 'Peregrine', his baptismal name. They thought it fitted better. Melissa liked that story too, but she liked it because she saw both in him, the hawk and the dove. He was fierce and intimidating at times, it was true, but there was also a tenderness and a quality of mercy about him that he had learned in the bitter school of suffering. 'Columba' had been a good choice, after all.

My name is Melissa. It is a family name. There has been a Melissa every now and then in our family for hundreds of years, since Abbot Peregrine's daughter. The last one before me was my mother's great-grandmother. She died the year I was born, and Mother didn't want the name to die out in our family, so I was christened Melissa too. I don't know what she'd have done if I'd been a boy.

The stories and the name were passed down through our family, grandmother to granddaughter, all the way to my mother's great-grandmother: hundreds of years. My mother's great-grandmother told them to my mother, and Mother loved the stories. She told them to me in my turn, when I was fifteen.

She waited until I was fifteen, because they were not children's stories. They were stories of men who had faced disillusionment and tasted grief and struggled with despair. Mother waited until I came to that time when I was no longer satisfied with the convenient and the pleasant and the comfortable; when I had seen enough of the shifting sands of appearances and wanted to stand firm on the truth, and then she began to tell me the stories that long ago Melissa had remembered and treasured about Abbot Peregrine, her father. He was an aristocrat, the son of a rich nobleman, and I must confess I liked that too: it's been a long time since we had one of those in our family. My own mother and father never had two ha'pennies to rub together, but that might have been because, with more faith than wisdom, they had five children.

When I was fifteen, my sister Therese was sixteen and my little sisters Beth and Mary were eight and six. My youngest sister Cecily was only three then, but she certainly made her presence felt. Daddy said she was like an infant Valkyrie, and words failed Mother to describe her adequately. She would just shake her head in silence. All three-year-olds are a force to be reckoned with when they get going, but I've never met anyone like my sister Cecily. She's not all that much different now, actually.

We lived in a small terraced house near the sea, which is the place my mind goes back to when I tell these stories, the stories Mother first told me there, the year I was fifteen. My sisters liked stories too, but not as much as Mother and I did. We lived with one foot in reality and one in fantasy, and sometimes we forgot which foot was which. I still do.

I went to school at a girls' High School. I have heard it said that 'schooldays are the best days of your life', but the best of my schooldays was the day I walked out of the gate for the last time and turned my back on it for ever. I used to feel as though my life was made up of weekends separated by deserts of weekdays, a bit like the beads on a rosary that come in clumps separated by bald stretches of chain. Perhaps I was a difficult person to teach—well, I know I was, they left me in no doubt about that—but if I gave my teachers trouble, it was nothing to the misery they caused me.

Have you ever been given one of those horrid joke presents, a big, inviting, exciting box, which when you open it contains only another box, and inside that another box, right down to the last one which has nothing at all inside? That's how my schooldays were. Day led onto day, a meaningless, hollow emptiness, the promise of learning no more than academic exercises wrapped around nothing.

I can see my headmistress' face now, the permed waves of grey hair rising from the domed forehead above those eyes that so remarkably resembled a dead cod, and the sort of embossed Crimplene armour she wore under her academic gown.

I learned very little. I have no idea where the Straits of Gibraltar are, and not until last weekend did I learn the square root of 900. But the day I opened the last package in the sequence and found it was an empty joke, I mean the day I pulled up the drawbridge of my soul forever, and never learned another thing from those teachers (though I was at the school two years more) was the day I got my English exam result. I was not good at many things at school, but I was good at English and I *knew* I was. I tried my best in the exam, and I hoped I'd done well. When the results were given out, I got 54 per cent, which just scraped a pass. I can remember it now, sitting in the classroom; the wooden desks with their graffiti, the high Victorian windows, and the teacher explaining to me that she had given me no marks at all for the content of my exam. She had given me marks for my punctuation and for my spelling, but that was all, because the content was, she felt, immoral. She had thought, she said, when she began to read it, that it was going to be a love story, but it turned out to be about God.

It seems funny (odd, I mean, not amusing) to think how that hurt me, then; how the shutters of my soul closed for good against the school that day. I know now what that poor, starved woman cannot have known, that not only my essay but the whole of life is a love story, about a tender and passionate God.

So my life was lived in the evenings and at weekends, and the greater part of my education was not geography or mathematics, but the wisdom my mother taught me, wrapped up in stories her great-grandmother Melissa had taught her.

Here are some of those stories.

CHAPTER TWO

Who's the Fool Now?

Stories and songs are for wet days and evenings, and for camping. You could offer me a mansion with central heating and every luxury; top quality stereo systems, colour televisions and ensuite bathrooms, and I would not exchange it for my memories of campfires under the stars.

I remember my little sisters, Mary and Beth and Cecily, dancing to the music of Irish jigs piped on a recorder, their silhouetted shapes leaping and turning in the firelight. I remember Mary's eager smile as she stretched up towards the flying sparks that floated high in the smoke. Fire-fairies, she said they were. I remember their breathless voices as they sang 'Father Abraham had many sons…', hopping and jumping the actions to the song.

Round the fire, sitting on the big stones that ringed it, were friends and family. Mother and Daddy, Grandma, my uncle and auntie, Grandad sitting in his camp chair with a pink towel draped over his head to stop the midges biting him. Familiar and commonplace in the daylight, as the dusk fell and night drew on they became folk tale figures, mythological beings from another age. The kindly light of the fireglow hid the irrelevances of whether Grandma's anorak was blue or white, or Auntie's trousers were fashionable, and revealed different things: the kindness of Grandad's face, and the serene wisdom of Grandma's. Daddy's face with its long beard looked like an Old Testament story all by itself. People think you can see more by electric light, but you can't.

You see different things, that's all. You can see to read or do your homework or bake a cake by electric light, but you see people more truly by candlelight and firelight. 'Technology is man-made, and has no soul,' my mother used to say.

'You're a pyromaniac!' Daddy would say to her. 'Candles, bonfires, campfires, fires on the hearth at home. Why can't we have central heating like everybody else?'

'Everybody else? Who's that?' Mother would reply. 'If there really is a faceless grey "they" mumbling, "There's safety in numbers," what is that worth to me? I need fire and earth and wind and waves as much as I need food. I'd go mad living in this wired-up, bricked-up, fenced-in concrete street if I didn't dose myself with fire and weather and earth and sea. My soul would get pale and thin. I don't want a pale, thin soul.'

'Okay.' Daddy knew when to give in. 'No central heating.'

Our camping holiday was an important part of our dose of the elements. We used to go to a place in the Yorkshire hills, sheltered by tall, whispering trees, beside a shallow stream where brown trout swam among the stones under the dappling of sunlight shining through leaves.

Sometimes the sun shone and we lay out on the grass reading comics and books, eating peaches and French bread and chocolate. Sometimes it rained and we lay in bed at night listening to the drumming of raindrops on the canvas, careful to let nothing touch the edge of the tent. On rainy days we warmed ourselves up with mugs of tea and chips from the chip shop, and watched, as the clouds cleared, the beauty of the wet hills holding the transparent, washed loveliness of the light like cupped hands holding the eucharist.

You don't see rainfall in a town. Oh, you can see that it's raining and you can get wet all right, but there is not the space to see the mist of rain blowing, the approach of rainfall across a valley, the majestic breadth of the sky with its gathering fleet of clouds. In the town, it is sunny or it is not. It is cold or it is warm. The gold of autumn and the silver of the rain has no meaning. Where I live now, I have a view from the front of my house of a large rendered wall painted grey, its flat surface relieved by an extractor fan, a flat blue door and a small window. From the back I can see a clutter of washing lines, sheds and greenhouses. But I remember the holidays of my girlhood by the stream and under the stars, and I still do as Mother did and take regular doses of fire and water, earth and air, to stop my soul getting pale and thin.

Daddy always said there was not much difference between camping and staying at home for us, because we girls slept on mattresses on the floor at home, too. Five of us children in a two-bedroomed house made mattresses a practical option. On winter nights we pushed them close together and kept each other warm. So camping had no sense of hardship or roughing it for us. Grandad brought his Tilley lamp and his calor gas camping stove, and Mother had her campfire in the evening.

We sat beside the fire one evening at camp, Mother and I. Daddy was putting the three little ones to bed, telling them the story of how the sky fell on Chicken Licken, and Therese had gone with Grandma and Grandad to buy some milk. It must have been early on in the week, because I don't think Uncle and Auntie were there that night.

'You haven't told me a story about Father Peregrine and the monks for ages,' I said. It was a clear, warm night and we had spent the early part of the evening gathering brushwood and fallen branches from among the trees, for the fire which was going beautifully now.

'I haven't, have I? All right then. Let me think a moment.'

✠ ✠ ✠

You remember Brother Thomas? Remember how, when Father Peregrine had been beaten and crippled, his hands maimed and broken, he struggled so hard to keep his fear and horror and grief hidden inside, and almost did; but it was Brother Thomas who plucked up the courage to put his arms round him and gave him the jog he needed to spill his grief, his misery and despair? Brother Thomas never forgot it either. He kept the memory in the tender, mysterious place at the very centre of his soul, and he had never spoken about it, because none of us can speak easily about the things that lodge in the very heart of us like that. He admired and respected his abbot for his justice and his natural authority and he loved him for the gentleness and mercy that was in him too. But at the very core of his love was the memory of Father Peregrine sobbing out his despair—'Oh God, how shall I bear the loss of my hands?'—as Brother Thomas held him in his arms.

Well this story concerns Brother Thomas, although most people called him Tom. Even Father Peregrine did in the occasional unguarded moment. Brother Tom was, as you remember, a vital and hearty young man, who hugged life in a mighty embrace and was given more to laughter than to tears. He had a deep appreciation of wine, women, song and good food, and he found the life of a monk very, very hard—at times intolerably hard. None the less, he loved the Lord Jesus to the bottom of his soul and was determined enough to follow his calling. But he did wonder, at times, if God should ever ask of him that he be removed elsewhere, to serve over the sea, or in another monastery, whether he could bear to leave his abbot, because although it was God who called him to the monastic life, it was Father Peregrine who kept him at it, or that was the way Brother Tom saw it. Then again, as he told himself, God's will was for him to serve in *this* monastery *here*, so maybe loving his superior was part of loving God, although... but here Brother Tom's brain wearied of the complications of the issue: he loved his abbot, and he understood his vulnerability as well as his strength. Truly, the two of them had been through some harrowing times together. In the course of Brother Tom's novitiate there had been an unfortunate incident with a young lady, which is a story all of its own, and had it not been for the way Father Peregrine dealt with Brother Tom and pleaded for him with the ancients of the community, Tom would have been turned out for good. Indeed, love his abbot though he might, Brother Tom caused him more trouble than all the others put together. He was on more than one occasion in disgrace for raiding the larder under cover of night, and his irrepressible streak of mischief combined with Brother Francis' inventive sense of humour caused chaos and disapproval again and again.

Father Peregrine had so often to plead for him and bail him out, to admonish him, listen to him, talk things through with him, pray for him and have him beaten, that he wondered from time to time if it wouldn't have been better for Tom simply to call it a day, give up struggling against the grain to be Brother Thomas, and return to farming the land with the family who had grieved to give him up. It amazed them both when Brother Tom at last came to the end of his novitiate (which was twice as long as it should have been, because of the young lady) and the community agreed to receive him for life and he made his solemn vows. Father Peregrine, who did not trust Tom out of his sight for too long, gave him the job of being the abbot's esquire, his own personal attendant. Brother Tom cleaned his house for him, waited on him at table, and did for him those tasks that his broken hands could not accomplish, for example, shaving him, buckling his belt, and fastening his sandals and tunic. Things went reasonably well for a while after he took his vows. The consideration that he was now a fully professed Benedictine monk had a sobering effect on Brother Tom, and he spent nearly six weeks after his solemn profession affecting an unnatural dignity that made Father Peregrine smile, and drew derision from Brother Francis who had made his own life vows three months previously and was now recovered from the awe and apprehension that went with it.

It didn't last. As inevitably as the flowering of bluebells in the spring came the temptations of the flesh that regularly assailed

Brother Thomas. After a week of fasting and praying, and scourging himself mercilessly in the privacy of his cell, he stole the key to the cellar, sat down by the biggest cask of wine he could find and got blind drunk. Brother Cormac discovered him there, and attempted to remonstrate with him, unwisely as it turned out, for black gloom had descended on the miscreant by then and Brother Cormac got nothing but a bloody nose for his pains. Brother Andrew, Cormac's superior in the kitchen, reported the matter to Father Peregrine in bristling indignation, and Father Peregrine, mortally weary of Tom's misdemeanours and exasperated beyond measure, had them souse him with a bucket of cold water and lock him up in the abbey prisons to sober up overnight.

Red-eyed, sneezing and penitent, Brother Thomas was brought to stand before the Community Chapter Meeting in the morning and receive his penance, which in these rare and unhappy circumstances was the standard one of a flogging.

Father Peregrine hated to see a man flogged, and he was upset as well as angry with Brother Tom, so spoke with more heat than he might normally do as Brother Thomas knelt down before him: 'Brother Thomas, you are a *fool*. You have the goodwill of this community and you *spit* on it. You have the trust of this community and you throw it away. You're a fool, Brother, because goodwill does not last for ever. You betray our trust, you betray your vocation, you betray the good name of this house with your silly capers. You are a fool!'

He glared at Brother Tom, and Tom humbly bent his aching head before his abbot's wrath. Both of them felt sick at heart, because in each of them the love for the other hurt like a splinter, like a sharp thorn. Father Peregrine was angry with Tom because he loved him, because he wanted him to be true to his vocation, because he didn't want to give the word to have him flogged. And Tom was ashamed and miserable because he'd failed again, because his abbot had spent so much time and kindness on him and he'd let him down once more.

Brother Clement, chosen for the job because he worked in the scriptorium and library, and therefore had little to do with Brother Tom and was as impartial towards him as any of the brothers could be, stood with the scourge in his hand. Brother Tom unfastened his tunic and undershirt, and bent low as he knelt before them, exposing his back to be beaten. Peregrine sat in his stall, his eyes downcast, the slight frown of distress that he could not help belying the sternness of his face.

'Father...' Brother Clement hesitated. Brother Tom's back was already a mass of purple welts where he had used the scourge savagely on himself in his battle against temptation.

'Ah, no!' said Peregrine, seeing it. 'Let that be finished with, Brother. No, no, I've no stomach to lay wound upon wound. Let him be. Resume your place, Brother Thomas. For your penance you may eat only dry bread and water these three days, and that you must take on your knees in the refectory, set apart from the brethren.'

It was on the third of these three days that Brother Tom came in to the abbot's lodging to sweep the floor and generally tidy up, and found Father Peregrine seated at his table, thoughtfully gnawing his lip as he frowned at a letter he was holding in his hand. He glanced up briefly at Brother Tom, grunted a response to Tom's pleasant 'God give you good day, Father', and went back to the perusal of his letter.

Brother Tom, as he swept the room, watched out of the corner of his eye as his abbot laid the letter down at last, and sat deep in thought for a while, then picked it up again and looked at it once more. It was written in an elegant hand on the finest vellum.

'The cunning devil!' Peregrine announced suddenly. 'Here, read this, Brother. 'Tis from Prior William of St Dunstan's Priory. You know, the Augustinian house. He invites me, in terms of the most friendly courtesy, to take part in a conference—a debate— concerning the nature of God, whether his supreme manifestation be in justice or in mercy.'

23

'What's wrong with that?' asked Tom, reaching out his hand for the document.

'Only that he hates me like poison, and that St Dunstan's Priory is three days' ride to the southwest, and his conference begins in three days' time. If Prior William bids us to conference he's up to no good somewhere. It's not like him to waste the substance of his house on hospitality if he can help it, and he doesn't intend me to be there for sure. It means leaving on the instant and riding half the night to be there in time. Why this sudden interest in the mercy and justice of God in any case? It never troubled his mind before that I recall.

'No... he's up to something and he counts on my absence to work it. He's a manipulator of minds and a good politician, but he's no theologian. Whatever he's cooking up, he wants me out of it because he knows I'll have the better of him in theological debate.'

He sat frowning in thought a while longer as Tom scanned the letter, then he exclaimed, 'No, I don't trust him! We'll go. I want to know what he's hatching.'

Brother Tom looked up from the letter in surprise. 'But Father, how are you going to—I mean, can you... ?'

'Sit on a horse without falling off? Yes? Well, we shall see, shan't we? Find Father Chad and Brother Ambrose. Have three horses saddled, prepare for ten days' absence. Make haste. Yes, you're coming with me. I don't trust you out of my sight, you drunken fool.'

The preparations were quickly made. It was agreed that Father Chad, the prior, should travel with them, leaving Brother Ambrose, the wise old cellarer, who was also the sub-prior, to rule over the community in their absence.

Brother Peter, who cared for the horses, considered Father Peregrine's situation carefully.

'You've been a good enough horseman, it'll not matter about your hands, but can you grip with your thighs? These two years

24

near enough you've been limping about on a crutch. Your muscles will be wasted. Not only that, but that stiff knee. I'm not sure... . Better not to arrive plastered in mud, I would imagine. How do you feel about being tied to your saddle? No, don't answer that. I can see by the look in your eye how you feel about it. Would it not be for the best though, truly?'

They did in the end strap him to his saddle as well as they could, and by noon they were on the road. They rode late into the night, that first night, slept under the stars in the lee of a hedge, and were on the road again before first light. The second night they begged food and lodging of a house of Poor Clares, who received them with warmth and kindness. They ate a hearty meal in the guest house there, and finished just in time to join the sisters for Compline. As they made their way to their beds, Brother Tom broke the Great Silence to whisper, 'Shall I not attend to your hands before you go to your bed, Father? Brother Edward has given me some oil, and said I mustn't forget to massage them every day. I neglected to do it yesterday. Will I not see to them tonight?'

Peregrine shook his head. 'Not now. We are in silence, and we need all the sleep we can get. We must be away early. Thank you, but leave it.'

'Father...'

'Leave it. We are in silence.'

With a sigh, Tom abandoned the conversation. He knew his abbot well and had seen how his proud spirit had balked at being tied to his horse like baggage on a mule. Peregrine had been touchy, on his dignity, all day, and was not about to have his independence eroded any further. He carried himself stiffly, and Tom guessed how the lame leg must be aching. Father Peregrine had not ridden since his leg bone was smashed. He looked weary. Tom glanced at him anxiously and tried one last plea: 'Father...'

'No.'

And they went to bed.

The kindly sisters made them a food parcel for their journey, and they were on their way directly after Mass. They had made such good time the first two days that they were assured of arriving at St Dunstan's before Vespers. Brother Tom and Father Chad rode side by side, enjoying the change of scenery and each other's company. Father Peregrine kept a little apart from them, speaking rarely and clearly on edge. They stopped to eat and water their horses at noon, and sat awhile to let the horses crop the roadside grass.

'Father, shall I not see to your hands?' Brother Tom ventured again.

Three days of holding the reins of a horse had left them more awkward than ever, and it had not escaped Tom's notice that it was with more difficulty than usual that Father Peregrine broke his bread and meat as they ate.

'Not now. We must press on. I want to be there before evening. Prior William is a heartless, cunning fox. Whatever this conference is about, it'll not be what it seems. He feels obliged to invite me to give credibility to his appearances, but see how he's left it so late that I can reasonably be expected to get there late or never, without actually being able to say I was not asked in time. Depend upon it he'll force me out of the debate in Chapter, and away from the meal table conversation if he can. Well, we shall see.'

'He knows then, does he, that you can't—that you no longer—that you are thus disabled, Father?' enquired Father Chad.

'Not from me, but yes, no doubt he knows. The only thing that takes more care to inform itself than love is hatred, and he hates me with a thoroughness that unnerves me a little, I confess. I've worsted him in debate before, and that he will not forgive. Anyway, enough, we must be away. We'll not be late.'

They rode in at the large grey stone gatehouse that straddled the moat surrounding the impressive priory of St Dunstan, just after the afternoon office, dusty and tired. They were received with all civility, and news of their arrival was sent to Prior William, who came out to meet them as their horses were led away to be stabled and rubbed down.

Prior William greeted first Father Peregrine, then Father Chad with the kiss of brotherhood. Brother Tom, who carried their pack, he barely acknowledged. As the formalities of greeting were exchanged, Tom studied the prior's face. Narrow, mobile and intelligent, with thin lips and very little colour, its most striking feature was his eyes, which were of a very pale blue beneath silver eyebrows. The premature whiteness of his hair added to the impression he gave of coldness and austerity. Tom reflected that though his lips curved in a smile as he addressed Father Peregrine, his tone as he spoke was like frostbite.

'A chamber is being prepared for you upstairs in the north wing of the guest house, Father Columba,' he said. His voice was as soft as a woman's; as soft as velvet.

'Upstairs?' butted in Brother Tom. 'My lord, there must be some mistake.'

'Let it be, Brother,' said Father Peregrine quickly, but Prior William's attention was caught.

'Is that inconvenient, my son?' he asked, in his soft, gentle, dangerous woman's voice. He turned to look at Brother Tom as he spoke, and Tom had a sudden feeling of panic, like a small, tasty animal caught in the predator's hypnotic death stare.

'He's—he's lame, my lord, as you see,' Tom stuttered.

'I had thought,' the prior purred, smiling faintly, 'that a man who could make such good time on horseback must be less disabled than I expected.'

Father Peregrine and Father Chad said nothing, but Tom was on his mettle now.

'If that be so, my lord,' he said, 'why did you not send him word earlier?'

The eyelids flickered momentarily over the cold blue eyes, but the prior did not stop smiling.

27

'Shall I instruct my men to prepare your chamber at ground level then?' he asked, fixing his gaze on Peregrine. Peregrine's face was grim as he met Prior William's look. Like an eagle confronting a poisonous snake, thought Tom.

'No, thank you,' said Father Peregrine. 'The upstairs chamber will do well.'

Prior William raised one sardonic eyebrow. 'If you are sure, my brother,' he murmured.

'I am sure,' said Father Peregrine. 'Please let us not detain you, Father Prior. I remember the way to your guest house well enough.' The two men bowed courteously to one another, and Prior William turned his attention to another small party of men who were riding in at the gatehouse, while Father Chad, Father Peregrine and Brother Tom made their way to their lodging.

'Father... forgive my asking...' Father Chad hesitated, daunted by the grimness of his abbot's look.

'Yes?'

'Forgive my asking you—how *are* you going to get up the stairs?'

'Backwards,' said Peregrine tersely. 'Unobserved, please God,' he added, with a flicker of a smile.

The stone stairway of the guest house was narrow and steep, but did not pose any great problem. Father Peregrine ascended it sitting on the steps, using his good leg to move him up one at a time, while Father Chad held the wooden crutch and Brother Tom carried their baggage. Tom could not help the grin that spread across his face at the undignified procedure, and Father Chad rebuked him. 'Brother, for shame, it is nothing to laugh at.'

But Peregrine smiled. 'Don't scold him, Father Chad. There'll be little enough to laugh at these four days if I judge right.'

Father Peregrine would not eat that evening with the company gathered after Vespers at Prior William's table, though he insisted that Father Chad and Brother Tom go.

'Keep your wits about you, listen to what's said and note

who's here. I'll see you later. I'll sup on the remains of the bread and meat the good sisters packed us for the road. I'm too stiff and sore to keep company.'

Tom took a deep breath. 'Father, *please*, when we return, will you permit me to see to your hands?' He looked in appeal at Peregrine, and somewhere in his gut, compassion clutched him as he read the look on his abbot's face, saw how his sense of dignity was cornered and mocked by his helplessness.

'Thank you,' said Peregrine quietly. 'If you would. I can scarcely move them.'

'After supper, then,' said Tom, cheerfully, and turned to follow Father Chad out of the room.

'Brother.' His abbot stopped him. 'You are quite welcome to say "I told you so".'

Tom grinned at him, understanding how fragile was the dignity with which he protected his disability. 'I wouldn't dare,' he replied. 'I wouldn't dare.'

✠ ✠ ✠

Most of the men who sat round the long, carved table in Prior William's great hall that evening were unknown to Brother Tom, but Father Chad discreetly pointed them out.

'Abbot Hugh from the Cistercian House to the east of our place, you know already. That's his prior with him, whose name I forget. The dark, bearded man I know not, though judging by his habit he's one of us. The slight, nervous fellow beside him is Abbot Roger, a Cistercian from Whitby.'

'Who is he?' asked Tom, nodding his head towards an enormously fat Benedictine monk, whose clean-shaven chins shook with laughter as he listened to a story his neighbour was telling him.

'He? Do you not know him? He has stayed with us before. It is the Abbé Guillaume from Burgundy. He has known Father

Abbot since childhood, I believe, and esteems him highly. An incomparable scholar and a wise and holy confessor.'

'Mmm. Good trencher-man too, by the look of him,' observed Brother Tom.

There were in all seven superiors of prestigious houses seated round the table. Father Robert Bishopton, the Cistercian from Fountains Abbey was there, and the abbot of St Mary's in York. Three of them had brought their priors too, and there were half a dozen other monks of less elevated status, but of scholarly renown—rising stars. So there was a good company gathered round the magnificent oak table.

Prior William's eyes rested meditatively on Father Chad and Brother Tom, and he drew breath as if to speak to them, but thought better of it and merely smiled at them, inclining his head in greeting. Thereafter he ignored them. They were glad of each other's company, neither of them being much at ease among the learned and the great. They were weary, too, from three days' hard riding and it was a relief when the meal was ended, Compline sung and they could turn in for the night. When they returned to their room in the guest house, Father Peregrine wanted to know just who was there and what was said. He heard their account of the company as Brother Tom worked over his hands, gently flexing and stretching the stiff fingers, probing and rubbing the cramped muscles. He listened, and then said, puzzled, 'I still don't understand why Prior William has summoned men of this calibre here to debate whether God's mercy is greater than his justice or the other way about. If it had been Abbé Guillaume I could have understood it. The night could pass and the sun come up and he never notice if he was absorbed in debating the things of God, but Prior William... they bear the same name, but you could hardly find two men less alike. Ah, what's he up to? I'd give my right hand to know. Not that I'd be missing much. Thank you, brother, you have eased them wonderfully. It takes a day or two to get them right again once I've let them get this bad. They don't ache so much though, now.' He yawned. 'Forgive me, brothers, you're falling asleep where you sit. To bed then.'

The august gathering met in the Chapter House after Mass the following morning, and there the day's business of the community was briefly despatched and the debate began.

It quickly became clear that Prior William, whatever his reasons, wanted the group of eminent men to conclude that God's justice outweighed his mercy. Brother Tom gazed around the room, drowsy with boredom as the men rose one by one to speak, citing the Church Fathers, the Old Testament and various Greek and Eastern philosophers he had never heard of. His attention was recaptured by Prior William's silky voice as he began to wind up the talk for the morning. 'It is on the cross that we see the final, ultimate vindication of God's justice, for God must remain true to his own laws, and requires a sacrificial victim for sin. His demand, yea thirst, for vengeance of his wrath aroused by our corruption requires a victim. Victim there must be, though it be his own Son. The price must be paid. Though the fruit of the cross is mercy, yet its root is justice, for it is a fair price paid, gold laid down for the purchase of our redemption.'

There was a silence at these words; a depressed, uneasy silence, broken by Abbot Peregrine's firm, quiet voice as he rose to his feet and stood leaning on his crutch, his hands hidden in his wide sleeves, his eyes fixed on Prior William's face.

'No, my brother, it is not so,' he said. 'The root of the cross is not justice, though its fruit be mercy, as you say. The root of the cross is love, and what is laid down is more than gold, it is blood, life: given not with the clink of dead metal, but with the groans of a man dying in agony. No yellow shine of gold, but the glisten of sweat, and of tears. Justice is an eye for an eye, and a tooth for a tooth, for every sin a sacrifice. But Christ, the sinless one, is he whose broken body suffered on the cross, and the holy God in Christ who suffered hell for our sin. That is more than

31

justice, my lord Prior, it is love. Nor is it merely a just love. It is a merciful love.'

He remained standing as Prior William rose to his feet to confront him. 'Are you suggesting,' purred the velvet voice, 'that God is not just?'

Peregrine shook his head. 'No. How should we know justice if God were not just? But I do say this: God's justice is subordinate to his love, for his justice is a property of his character, but his love is his essential self. For do not the Scriptures say, "God is love," but never, "God is justice"?'

Brother Tom had no idea which of them was right, if either, and was not sure what the point of the argument was anyway, but Prior William's smooth, disturbing voice, that spoke of victims and wrath and vengeance and gold and corruption, made him feel a bit sick. He felt on firmer ground with Father Peregrine's talk of suffering, merciful love, and to judge by the atmosphere of the meeting, he was not the only one.

Abbé Guillaume rose to speak, and the two men broke the look that locked them in combat and resumed their seats to hear him.

'Le bon Dieu, yes he is charité. But he is perfection, is he not? And is not perfection the essence of justice? The precise, appropriate purity of verité—n'est-ce pas? Is not justice as we conceive of it none other than that which approximates to perfection? Eh bien, in the incomprehensible perfection of God, where all is a radiance of pure light, all crookedness is made straight, is not love swallowed up in the manifestation par excellence of justice—that is perfection?'

'No!' Peregrine was on his feet again, his eyes burning. 'No, good brother. For God loves me, even me; and though Satan parades my sins and weakness before me, yet am I saved by the love of God in Christ Jesus, from which nothing can separate me. Justice would separate me from the love of God. By my sins do I justly perish. But I am redeemed, reborn, recreated; I am held and sheltered and restored by the love of God. Mon père,

I cannot call that justice. It is grace, free grace. It is the most prodigal generosity. It is all mercy.'

Brother Tom glanced across the Chapter House at Prior William. The prior was gently caressing his chin with his hand, and his eyes were fixed on Father Peregrine with a cold, calculating, thoughtful look. Tom had never before seen such pure hatred, unmixed with passion or anger or any such agitation. Ruthless, single hatred. He shivered. The company murmured assent to Peregrine's assertion, but Père Guillaume took it serenely. To him, winning or losing was immaterial. He saw debate as a lovely thing in itself, a sculpture of truth chiselled out by the cut and thrust of argument. He was well content.

It was at this point that the Chapter Meeting broke for High Mass, and Tom sighed with relief to be able to stretch his stiff limbs and move again. After the suffocating boredom of the morning's debate, the liturgy with its colour and music seemed like a night out at the inn. Despondency descended on him as they returned to the Chapter House to pursue the debate after Mass. He decided that four days of this would be more than he could endure, and resolved to make himself scarce after the midday meal.

Meanwhile, the talk batted to and fro, concerning the perfection of justice, the perfection of mercy, the essence of perfection, whether or not perfect mercy is a form of justice, the essence of God—all substantiated by long quotations in Latin which Tom couldn't understand properly, and references to bits of the Athanasian Creed which he couldn't remember. Eventually he dozed off to sleep.

He cheered up considerably at lunch time. The table was laden with the choicest roast fowls in rich sauces, vegetables beautifully prepared, dishes of fruit and cheese—a feast to make a man's mouth water. The normal rule of silence was suspended on this occasion, so that the talk might continue on an informal basis. Brother Tom didn't care what they talked about. There was enough food here for him to eat as much as he wanted for once in his life, and as soon as the long Latin grace was said, he applied himself to it with great relish.

The men who sat down to eat were divided roughly according to status. Prior William presided at the head of his table among the scholarly and eminent men he had invited to conference. Lower down the table were those like Father Chad, men of importance but not of the first rank—abbots' priors mainly. Brother Tom sat with the small fry at the end of the table; young monks like himself who were their abbots' esquires. He felt a little uneasy at being separated from his abbot. Once again he had not had chance to attend to his hands, nor opportunity to speak to the lay brothers who served at table here, to ask them to help Father Peregrine with his food. Still, his abbot had common sense enough, and was used to coping with these situations. No doubt he would prefer to avoid having attention drawn to his disability.

Brother Tom investigated the wine that had been poured for him. Like him, the young men among whom he was seated were used to watered ale at table, and his neighbour turned to him with a smile of pure contentment as he set down his elegant, silver goblet. 'That,' he said, 'is like the fire in the heart of a ruby. I think I could find a vocation to this community with very little persuading.' It *was* good wine, clear and dark and smooth. A glow of well-being spread through Brother Tom.

'Faith, yes, I could see off a barrel of this,' he replied happily. 'But it would take more than that to tempt me to live my life in the chill of that miserable icicle of a man.'

His neighbour laughed and glanced up the table towards Prior William. 'Endearing, isn't he? Never mind, he knows where to purchase his victuals. Have you tried this cheese?'

Though there was a fair number of men there, they were used to eating in silence; not only without talk, but without unnecessary scrape and clatter. Their conversation was a discreet

34

hum of sound, and it was easy enough for Prior William to raise his smooth, soft voice just sufficiently loud to be heard by all the company: 'Ah... I crave your pardon, Father Columba. It had never occurred to me that the mutilation of your hands would render you so... incapable. What an oversight! You are used perhaps to having your food cut up for you?'

Brother Tom's hand stopped halfway to his mouth and slowly sank down to his plate again. The morsel of cheese he was holding dropped from his fingers forgotten. He watched Peregrine's mortification as the attention of the whole table was inevitably turned towards him. He had spilt some of his food, but not much, and had been struggling with his knife to cut a piece of meat. It was unwise to attempt it, but he was hungry and the food was delicious. The knife had turned in his awkward grasp, and there was gravy splashed on his hands and on the fine linen tablecloth. Brother Tom looked anxiously at Prior William as he reclined in his graceful chair, holding Peregrine in the cool taunting of his gaze.

'Don't,' whispered Tom. 'Oh, please don't.' It was unbearable.

'Perhaps you would prefer to have your food cut up for you?' purred the spiteful voice. The pale eyes watched him relentlessly. The eyebrows were raised and the lips curved in their mirthless smile. Father Peregrine returned his gaze, his face flushed, his jaw clenched. The men nearest them stirred uncomfortably and tried in vain to keep their conversation going.

Father Peregrine looked down a moment at his food. Then he looked back at Prior William. The pale blue eyes shone with malicious mockery. 'Father Columba?' he prompted. Brother Tom held his breath.

'Yes, please,' said Peregrine humbly. 'I would be grateful for that assistance.'

Tom's breath sighed out of him as the tension was broken. He felt like standing on his chair and cheering. 'What a man! What a man! To so humble himself to that cruel devil!' he rejoiced inside.

But his rejoicing was numbed when he saw how Peregrine's hand was shaking as he reached out for his goblet of wine. It had cost him dear.

'Oh! Alas!' came the hateful, gentle voice again. 'Father Columba has spilt his wine now. You do normally feed yourself, Father? I never thought to ask.'

'I do,' said Peregrine, almost inaudibly.

'Ah well, never mind,' the prior's voice persisted. 'The boy will mop up the mess you have made. Boy! See the mess he has made: there… yes and there. And there. Thank you. Replenish his wine.'

The cut food was replaced in front of Father Peregrine, and he murmured his thanks but scarcely touched it after that. His wine he drained like medicine, and he drank heavily throughout the rest of the meal, speaking to no one, his confidence shattered. And all the while, those pale, malevolent eyes returned to look at him complacently. The company rose from their meal in time for the afternoon office of None. Peregrine swayed as he tried to stand, and leaned on the table for support. Brother Tom hastened to his side.

'Are you not well, Father Columba?' came the heartless voice. 'Perhaps you have taken a little too much wine? We shall quite understand if you wish to be excused from the Office.'

'Oh shut up,' muttered Brother Tom under his breath, and he took his abbot's arm and looked round for Father Chad.

Between them, he and Father Chad manoeuvred their abbot and his crutch out of the prior's house and back across the cloister to the guest house. They were kindly ignored by the other guests, and Brother Tom was relieved to catch a glimpse out of the corner of his eye of Prior William departing for chapel.

'Now for the stairs,' said Father Chad dubiously, as they came to the guest house door. Peregrine raised his head.

'Chad, go to chapel,' he ordered abruptly. 'I don't trust that weasel out of my sight and hearing. Go to chapel. I'll join you later.'

But he leaned on Brother Tom as he spoke, and his speech was very slurred. Tom doubted very much if he would be going anywhere but his bed, although getting him there would be another matter.

Some of his escapades with Brother Francis proved good practice for this occasion for it was not easy manhandling a man, both lame and dead drunk, backwards up the narrow stairway. Peregrine complicated matters by refusing point-blank to relinquish his crutch, which he clung to as the last symbol of his independence.

They made it though, and Tom helped him into his chamber, where he collapsed onto a chair and sat staring moodily at nothing.

'Let me unfasten your boots, Father. I think maybe a sleep would do you good,' suggested Brother Tom, and squatted at Peregrine's feet to untie the thongs that laced his boots.

Resting his hand on his abbot's knee, he looked up into his face at the bleary, unfocused eyes and uncharacteristic sag, and could not resist a grin. 'Faith, man, you have drunk well,' he said. Peregrine looked at him morosely, and nodded in assent.

'Who's the fool now?' he said bitterly.

But Tom's look of amusement and affection penetrated the fog of alcohol and misery that enveloped him, and he managed a lopsided smile.

Brother Tom coaxed him into his bed, where he slept like the dead until morning.

✠ ✠ ✠

The next day, in the Chapter meeting, Father Peregrine was determined to make up for the ground he had lost by his absence from the previous afternoon's debate. Père Guillaume spoke of all the Old Testament history in which God's justice was the sign of his presence, the manifestation of his love. He spoke with impressive and detailed knowledge, and Prior William sat nodding with satisfaction in his chair as he heard him. But when Peregrine stood to speak, their eyes were all upon him. His absence had not gone unremarked the day before, and the men were curious to know what he would say now; how he would conduct himself, having last left their midst too drunk to walk alone.

'It is true, what you say, Abbé Guillaume,' he said. 'It is true that judgement and authority, the instruments of justice on earth, are authenticated by the command of God. It is true that God shapes the lives of men in the ways of justice, and that the righteous find expression of his Spirit in the paths of justice and of peace. But justice is a path, yes a way; it is not a home. It is a framework, or a setting, but it was made to carry another jewel. Justice, like John the Baptist, is the forerunner, clears the road, for the coming of the Christ himself. And when he comes, he is compassion. He is love. Remember the words of the psalmist *"Hodie si vocem ejus audientis, nolite obdurare corda vestra."* Harden not your hearts. Today, if you want to hear the Lord's voice, harden not your hearts. Oh God forbid that our lives display the sterile correctness of men who have learned what justice is, but never tasted mercy.'

The gathering of men listened spellbound to the urgency of his voice, as he clung like a terrier to a rat to his insistence on God's merciful love as the one, central, all-supporting fact of life.

The prior watched him without emotion, biding his time. In debate this man was magnificent, but he was not invulnerable, it seemed. There were other ways of discrediting him. Prior William smiled complacently as they went in to eat after the midday Office. He waited his moment with pitiless detachment. There was entertainment to be derived from seeing this accomplished and scholarly aristocrat grow increasingly uneasy as he tried to ignore the sadistic patience of his host, tried not to lose his nerve under that unpleasantly speculative gaze. There was pleasure in the waiting, but not too long. Once grace was said, the men were seated and the meal was underway, the cruel, gentle voice began.

'Oh, but we mustn't forget to cut your food up for you, Father

Columba. Ah, it is done. Can you manage—or not really? Alas, how thoughtless of me to provide insufficiently for you. Look, Father Columba, you have dropped a piece of meat. It seems a shame to soil your garments so, does it not? Perhaps you should have a towel tied about you, as a child does who is learning to eat, yes? That would answer your requirements, would it not? Fetch a towel, boy, a large one, and tie it about him.'

The conversation at the head of the table had ceased in the embarrassment of this baiting, and the men occupied themselves self-consciously with their food. Father Peregrine withdrew his hands from sight and hid them in his lap, protected from view by the wide sleeves of his habit. Mute and still, he waited for the next gibe as the boy came towards him with the towel, and Prior William leaned forward to speak again, his victory shining softly in his eyes.

'Mais non, laissez-le tranquil, mon père. Ca suffit,' murmured Abbé Guillaume unhappily, but the prior did not heed him.

'Thanks, lad. There now, here is the towel. Shall he not tie it about you, my friend?'

Peregrine looked round at the boy standing there with the cloth in his hands and then at the sophisticated men who sat hushed in unwilling fascination at the sight of him caught in his clumsiness and helplessness. It was more than he could bear.

'No!' The harsh pain of his cry splintered the tension of the atmosphere. Tom thought the loneliness of it would have bruised a heart of stone, but it did nothing to disturb Prior William's placid smile. He scarcely even blinked. Peregrine groped on the floor for the crutch that lay beside him, and pushing back his chair with a violence that sent it crashing to the ground, he stumbled blindly to the door. One of the serving-boys assisted him in his ineffectual struggle with the latch, and he escaped.

Brother Tom sat frozen in his seat, appalled. The prior looked down the length of the table at him, his eyebrows raised, his eyes mocking. 'He seems a temperamental, unstable man, your lord,' he remarked in the silence. 'Does he ever complete a meal both sober and in good humour? Or have I said something to upset him?'

The blood was pounding in Tom's ears like thunder. He stared, speechless with rage, at this cruel, smiling man. His heart remembered those weeping words from long ago, 'Oh God, how shall I bear the loss of my hands?'. And he lost his temper.

Slowly, he rose in his place. Father Chad took one look at him and buried his head in his hands. Brother Tom walked with measured deliberation to the head of the table, and stood looking down at the prior, who returned his look with scornful amusement.

Tom took a deep breath, and with an effort kept himself from shouting. 'It is easy, easy, sir,' he said, his voice unsteady with restrained rage, 'to humiliate a man and make him look foolish. Why, all it takes is this...' Quick as lightning, Tom shot out his arm, seized the prior by his silver hair and smacked his head down into his dinner. He stood shaking with anger, oblivious to the murmurs of some and the stunned silence of others. Prior William lifted his dripping face from the table. His left eyebrow was decorated with a blob of parsley sauce. The boy who held the towel hurried to his side.

'It's not so easy to win a debate, nor to humble yourself before another man!' Tom bellowed at him. 'That takes intellect and courage. You, my lord, have made it plain that you have neither!' He stood glaring at him for a moment, then said in contempt, 'Ah, you sicken me. I would rather be the cockroach that crawls on the floor in the house where my abbot is master than be the greatest of those who serve under you.'

It might even then not have been so bad had not Father Roger from Whitby added a quiet 'Amen'. That was the last straw.

'Take him away,' snapped Prior William, his face a mask of fury behind the remnants of sauce. 'Let him cool his head in the prisons until his master is in a fit state to give permission for his flogging. I had heard the Benedictine houses were sliding into decadence, but now I see it with my own eyes.'

It was not until after the afternoon's discussions had been concluded and Vespers said that Father Peregrine caught up with Father Chad.

'Where's Brother Thomas?' he asked, with some trepidation. 'What's he done now?'

'I regret he made a spectacle of himself at the table after you left, Father.' Father Chad shook his head sadly. 'He pushed my lord prior's face down into his dinner. He said it took no more than that to humiliate a man and make him look foolish. He said it took courage to humble oneself before another man, and intellect to win a debate, and that my lord prior had neither. His implication was that you, Father, have both, though he left that unsaid.'

He raised his face to look at his superior, sorry and ashamed, but Peregrine was grinning at him incredulously.

'He did so? He said that? Well God bless him. That redeems a few insults. Courage to humble oneself and intellect to win in debate. And I was about to run away. What have they done with him then?'

'He was confined in the prison, Father, until you should be with us again to give permission for his flogging.'

'Flogging for what? Not I! They'll not lay a finger on him!'

✠ ✠ ✠

The confrontation came in the Chapter meeting the following morning, as part of the business before the theological debate. Brother Tom, dishevelled and defiant, was brought to stand before the gathering to face the prior enthroned on his high-backed, intricately-carved chair on its dais. Prior William regarded him with cold dislike (as much charity as a man bears towards the slug on his salad, thought Tom).

41

'You deserve to be flogged, you young fool,' said the suave, smooth voice, 'for your gross and brutish manners. You give your permission, I am sure, Father Columba, for his beating?'

The velvet voice permitted itself a shade of triumph. He had caught them. Disgraced them. Discredited them. But Father Peregrine replied, 'I do not.' He rose to his feet. 'In my house,' he said, 'we do not flog a man for loyalty, nor for love, however inadvisedly expressed. We treasure it. However, neither do we permit discourtesy and violence to go unchecked. Brother Thomas, you must ask his forgiveness.'

Brother Tom looked at his abbot, who returned his look calmly, confident of his authority with his own. Tom knelt before the prior.

'Father, I humbly confess my fault of grave discourtesy and unseemly violence. I ask God's forgiveness for my offence, and yours, my lord.'

Prior William looked down at Brother Tom, his pale eyes bulging with rage. He had no idea how they'd done it, but they'd turned the tables on him somehow. For how can you humiliate a man who humbles himself, or disgrace a man who willingly kneels? There stood that insufferable cripple, with the bearing of a king, and there knelt his loutish boy, humbly begging forgiveness, with not even a trace of cynicism or rebellion to his voice that one could fasten on to condemn.

'You are forgiven. Go in peace,' the prior spat out, after the custom of his house. The beautiful words almost choked him. 'Go to hell' would have been more in line with the look on his face.

Peregrine spoke again. 'I recommend for your penance, my son, that you be returned to your cell, for it seems I cannot guarantee your self-control when you are provoked to anger. I suggest you fast there on bread and water until we return home.'

'So be it,' snapped the prior, and irritably dismissed Brother Tom with his long, white, bejewelled hand.

So Tom finished the week as he had begun it, fasting on bread and water, in narrow escape of a severe beating. There were three prison cells, grim stone hovels, their only light the rays of the morning sun shining through the small barred window set in each of the heavy doors. In the cell adjoining his was one of the local men, a farmer, kept there until his family should pay off an outstanding debt to the priory, for right of way across the canons' land. He and Tom whiled away some of the hours of their imprisonment in talk. They could converse tolerably well if they raised their voices and stood with their faces up against the barred apertures in the cell doors.

'He's a grasping old tyrant, is the prior,' the farmer ruminated, when he had told Tom the story of his troubles and his debt. 'Well, that's plain enough. Look at this conference, up to his tricks again. "Enough" is a word beyond his understanding.'

'What? I thought this business was all theology, spiritual stuff.'

'Spiritual? God save us, nothing's spiritual here but the servants' wages. No, he wants the fishing rights of the river.'

'*Fishing?* What has that to do with his conference?' Tom was bewildered.

'Justice and mercy, isn't it, all this talk? Am I right? Ah, I thought so. Well, young man, justice, in Prior William's terms, is that all the fishing of the whole stretch of the river that runs through his lands, four miles of it, nigh on, is his. He can turn off any of the villagers who seek a little fishing there, and fine any poachers. Mercy means that a man of the cloth like him should look kindly on the rights the villagers have enjoyed for years, and let them have a little pleasure and a few fish dinners at his expense. Now then: which is a man of God? Just or merciful? Prior William's notion is to have justice win the day, so he can lean on the Bishop to back him up when he petitions the sheriff to enforce his fishing prohibition. Eh? Are you still there?'

'I'm here, but... stone the crows! The greedy old... ! Is it true what you say? *Fishing*!'

'Aye well, you monks eat a lot of fish.' The farmer chuckled appreciatively at Tom's indignant snort.

'Any road, that's the story. Eh up, here comes my vegetable broth and your dry bread. Mother of God, you must have almost a quarter pound there. Is it a feast day?'

✠ ✠ ✠

Father Peregrine also finished the conference lightheaded with hunger, surviving the nightmarish meals where, for the glory of God, he humbled himself to be tied in a towel like a child. He also finished triumphant in debate, having established beyond all doubt in the minds of his hearers what they should have known anyway, that it is mercy which is the power of God.

So Prior William, having spent hand over fist on hospitality to prove the opposite point, lost his case (he later had his suit rejected by the Bishop, and lost his fishing rights too). He did not come out to bid Father Peregrine farewell on the morning they left, Tom having been released from imprisonment, eaten heartily and shaved his abbot with loving care.

But as they rode out, Abbé Guillaume hailed them from across the court where his own party were making ready. He came running breathlessly.

'Adieu, mon frère,' he said, taking Peregrine's hand tenderly. 'It is an honour to have engagé in debate with you once more.'

Peregrine bent down in his saddle and gave the abbé the kiss of brotherhood. He stood, still clinging to Father Peregrine's hand, his chins quivering with emotion.

'*Qui se humiliaverit, exaltabitur, non?* The man who humbles himself is exalted. God will not forget. Moi non plus. Adieu.' And he kissed the twisted hand. Standing back from them he waved in salute.

'Adieu, Frère Thomas! Would I were loved by our young

brothers as well as your abbé is loved by you! Adieu, Père Chad! Au revoir!'

They rode home with almost the same urgency of their outward journey, thundering across the moorland turf of the last few miles, Peregrine longing for the haven of his own community. When they arrived, they were greeted by the porter opening the gate with the news that there were distinguished guests staying in the guest house, Sir Geoffrey and Lady Agnes d'Ebassier. Father Peregrine shook his head. 'Father Chad, you and Brother Ambrose must be their hosts tonight. I'm not eating with *anyone*—I'm too hungry.'

✠   ✠   ✠

Mother pushed the wood together on the fire. A little flame sprang up out of its dying glow. Sitting on the stone in the firelight, wrapped in a shawl, the folds of her blue skirt falling around her feet and her unruly hair tumbling down her back, she looked as though she didn't belong in this century any more than Peregrine did.

'That was a horrible, horrible man,' I said. '*Nobody* could behave like that.'

'Don't you think so?' She was still not satisfied with her fire, and rearranged it until it was burning well again. 'That's better.'

'Well, I've never met anyone like it.'

Mother sat crouched on her stone, her chin in her hand, watching the fire. The flames illuminated her face. Around us, dusk was deepening into night. 'Cruelty,' she said, turning her head to look at me, 'is part of human nature. An acorn is like an oak. The small, acceptable cruelties you and I might get away with are not much different from Prior William's spite.'

'How depressing,' I said gloomily. 'I don't want to be like him.'

'Well, that's all right. When you have no mercy to give, you can always ask for more. For all our cruelty and heartlessness there is a prayer, "Lord Jesus, have mercy on me, a sinner." His mercy takes root in us. Grows like a weed if you give him the chance. Where's your father? Not still putting Cecily to bed?'

'No, here he comes. Oh good, he's got a bottle of wine! And Therese has some crisps.'

Mother smiled and stretched out her feet to the fire's warmth. 'Songs and stories and wine by a campfire… people who stay in hotels don't know what they're missing.'

'Mother,' I said, as I reached my hand out for the plastic beaker of wine Daddy offered me, '—thank you, Daddy—what was that you said about Brother Tom and a young lady?'

'I said he got into trouble in his novitiate year, after he'd taken his first vows.'

'Will you tell me that story?'

'Some day. Not tonight. Remind me another evening.'

I did remind her, every evening we were at camp, but the little ones stayed up later and later, playing in the stream and singing songs round the fire, so there were no more stories until the holiday was over and we were home again.

CHAPTER THREE

Keeping Faith

Therese had finally been enlisted to help with the Sunday School. Mrs Crabtree had been trying for a long time to persuade her, and in the end she had given in.

She sat in our kitchen on Saturday morning with her feet up on a stool, the table strewn with papers, preparing a lesson for the seven- to ten-year-olds on the theme of friendship. When I came in to make myself a cup of coffee she was talking about it to Mother, who was sitting in the easy chair topping and tailing gooseberries for dinner.

'And what did they say?' Mother was asking as I came in.

'Lilian says a friend is someone who is always there when you need them. Daddy says a friend is someone you can trust. Susanne says a friend is someone who likes you. I've got down here, "A friend is someone you like being with." I can't remember who said that. Jo Couchman says a friend is someone who always understands. Beth says a friend is somebody you know. Mary says a friend is someone you play with.'

'Did you ask Melissa?'

'No, not yet. I'm asking everybody for my Sunday School thing, 'Lissa, what they think a friend is. What do you say?'

'A friend is… crumbs, let me think. Someone who sticks by you, I think. Someone who won't let you down.'

'That's good; thanks. Make me a cup of coffee, too, will you? Oh, Mother, you haven't said. What do you think a friend is?'

Mother frowned thoughtfully and carried on nipping the little stalks off her gooseberries without replying. She said eventually, 'Well... I've had friends who've disappointed me. Sometimes, even the ones who loved me have let me down, and not understood, and betrayed my trust. That's only human nature, isn't it? I daresay I've done as much to them. No, I would say... I learned it from a story great-grandmother Melissa told me... I would say that because we all have our failings and weaknesses, because each of us is only human, a friend—a good friend—is someone who helps you to persevere.'

'What?' said Therese.

'A friend is someone who helps you to persevere. When the going gets tough and you're on the point of jacking it all in; by the time you reach my age, Therese, you will be able to look back at lots of times when you nearly gave up and walked away from a difficult situation; and the people you will remember with thanks and love are the ones who helped you, in those moments, to persevere.'

'Okay, okay, I've got it; don't preach a sermon at me, Mother,' said Therese. 'A friend is someone who helps you to persevere. I bet they won't even know what "persevere" means.'

'Well if they don't,' said Mother drily, 'it's time they learned. It'll come in handy.' She finished her gooseberries and took them to the sink to wash.

'What was the story, then, Mother? Here's your coffee, Therese.'

Mother looked over her shoulder at me and smiled. 'Come for a walk after dinner, up on to the hill, and I'll tell you the story. There's not time now, and anyway I've got to make this pudding, which needs thinking about because I've never made it before.'

It was a warm, lazy day and Cecily fell asleep after dinner. Somebody needed to stay at home and mind her, and Daddy wanted to read the paper, so he was very glad of the excuse she gave him to stay at home. Mary and Beth went along the road to play in a neighbour's sandpit, and Therese was still struggling with her Sunday School lesson for the following day.

'Looks like just you and me then, Melissa,' Mother said after the dinner things had been washed up. 'Do you still want to go?'

'Course I do! I've been waiting for this story since before dinner!'

We took the dog and set off up the hill to where our road forked. Leaving the houses behind, we took the left-hand fork and followed the narrow unmade track to the heath at the top. It was a clear, warm day, and the breeze smelled of the sea. After five minutes' walking the sound of traffic was no more than a hum in the distance.

We were in a place of seagulls and gorse, rabbits and sea-pinks among the rocks and wiry grass.

We walked in silence up the hill; it was steep enough that you needed your breath for climbing and had none to spare for talking. Our dog ran ahead of us, his tail curled over his back, a flag of happiness. He trotted in zig-zags, his nose snuffing the track of rabbits along the ground.

As we breasted the rise of the hill, Mother paused to get her breath back and look out over the sea. The other side of the hill fell away sharply from the plateau of gorse and turf on the top; a cliff face that dropped down to the sea shore. From where we stood, we could see for miles. On the one side the pebbly beach lay below, where the fishing boats were drawn up and their nets spread to dry near the wooden shacks where the fishermen sold their catch. On the other side spread the patchwork of allotments, and the parish church, and the winding terraces of houses that clung to the hillside.

'Let's sit down here for a while,' Mother puffed. 'I'm still too full of dinner and it's too hot to walk far.'

We sat down on the grass near the gorse bushes at the cliff edge. Mother reclined on her elbow, shaking back her mane of hair. I noticed for the first time that it had strands of grey in it here and there.

'The story,' I prompted.

'Oh, just a minute, let me get my breath back!'

We sat there for a while, listening to the long pull of the surf, and the cry of the gulls overhead, watching the bees visiting the gorse flowers, industrious and content.

Then she began her story.

✠ ✠ ✠

Brother Francis finished off the little red dragon he had painted at the foot of the page. He had intended it to glower at the reader with an intimidating scowl from the margin of Psalm 102, 'For my days are consumed away like smoke and my bones are burnt up as it were with a firebrand... .' Francis looked doubtfully at his dragon, a perky little beast with an endearingly quizzical expression on its face. He didn't understand why Brother Theodore's illuminations reflected the passion and loveliness of the sacred text, but his own always managed to introduce a note of unseemly comedy. The problem was not restricted to the art of manuscript illumination either. Since first he had entered the community, Brother Francis' irrepressible cheerfulness had caused consternation to Father Matthew, the master of novices, who took his responsibility of watching over their souls with a seriousness bordering on obsession.

'I must answer for them before God,' he said earnestly to Father Peregrine. 'I must account for them on the judgement day. And how I shall account for Brother Theodore and Brother Thomas and Brother Francis, I do not know. I have rebuked them, exhorted them—"Brethren be sober, be vigilant, because your adversary the devil goeth about as a roaring lion, seeking whom he may devour!" And Brother Francis says to me, "Yes, Father Matthew," as if butter wouldn't melt in his mouth, but there is a twinkle in his eye and I can't get rid of it.'

Father Peregrine hoped desperately that there was no such

damning twinkle in his own eye, and did his best to adopt a suitably grave expression, but he couldn't be sure. The thing that was worrying Father Matthew above all else about Brother Francis was the way he walked.

'Have you seen him, Father?' he demanded of Peregrine, shaking his head in bewildered sorrow. 'He walks along the cloister with a step that is as merry and light as a Franciscan friar! It's not dignified, it's not edifying, it's not right.'

'He has a naturally sunny temperament, that's all,' Father Peregrine consoled his novice master, 'and I'm glad he's happy here.'

'But he shouldn't be so happy, that's just it. He should be reflecting on his sins and the awesome judgement of God. He came here to live a life of penance and prayer, not to enjoy himself.'

'And does he not pray?'

'Yes indeed, I have no complaints of his diligence in prayer or in work. On the contrary; but the more he prays, the worse he gets.'

Peregrine bent his head in an attempt to disguise the smile that tugged at the corners of his mouth.

'I think, Father Matthew, you worry yourself unnecessarily,' he said finally. 'Your conscientious vigilance will save him from much levity, and much mirth, I am sure.'

Father Matthew looked at his abbot with a glimmer of hope in his troubled eyes, 'Do you really think it might?'

'I am sure of it,' Peregrine replied solemnly, but there was something in his manner that caused a faintly suspicious look to cross the novice master's face. 'You don't think I am too hard on the novices, Father?'

'Well—now and again, maybe,' said Peregrine gently.

'But their souls, their young souls that are constantly tempted to sin!' Father Matthew leaned forward in his chair, his eyes glowing like coals.

'Yes... yes, I know. It's not easy.' Peregrine nodded sympathetically. 'They—we all—respect your devotion to God and to your duty, Father. But don't lose too much sleep over Brother Francis. I think his vocation is secure enough.'

Francis, who had no wish to cause offence to anyone, did his best to comply with Father Matthew's attempts to mould and discipline his character, and struggled to adopt an air of appropriately sober monastic recollection. The effect was more that of adding an easy urbanity to the original impish good humour; a sort of charming serenity which Father Matthew could never be sure was an improvement or the reverse.

Brother Clement, an artist and a scholar, in whose charge were the library and the scriptorium, had no fears for Francis' soul, but was frustrated by his manuscript illumination. He looked in vexation at Francis' alert and interested little dragon.

'Brother, the text you have copied well enough—your hand is not excellent, but it will do, it is passable. But this! Have you read the thing you are illuminating? Your purpose is to *illuminate*, not to obscure, the text. Here, where the psalmist says, "*Percussus sum ut foenum, et arnuit cor melim; quia oblitus sum comedere panum meum.*" Do you not know what that means? "My heart is smitten down and withered like grass so that I forget to *eat*." He goes on, "I lie awake and moan." The man is in pain, Brother Francis, not in fairyland.'

Francis looked chastened. 'I know,' he admitted. 'I didn't mean it to look like that. It was supposed to look threatening. I could do its eyebrows a bit blacker after the midday meal, perhaps.'

But the dragon was spared his cosmetic surgery, because after the midday meal Brother Dominic, the guestmaster, waylaid Brother Clement. 'Brother, I wonder if you could spare me a pair of hands from the scriptorium for the guest house? We're almost rushed off our feet there, what with Father Gerard laid up sick and a great party of folk that's just arrived today.'

Brother Clement's eyes brightened. 'I'll send you Brother Francis directly,' he replied.

That evening, the visitors from the guest house dined with Father Peregrine, as was customary. There were one or two travelling south to Canterbury on pilgrimage, and a family passing through who had asked for hospitality and help because one of their horses had gone badly lame. There were two little children in the family, who had been left tucked up asleep in the guest house, but the mother and father and their two older children supped with the abbot. Their eldest was a girl of sixteen, Linnet, a vivacious, pretty girl with dark brown eyes and rosy cheeks. She had glossy black hair coiled demurely in a net, wisps of it escaping to curl on her neck and brow. Her brother, four years her junior, excited and proud to be included in adult company, sat beside her, and they chatted happily to Brother Edward sitting opposite them.

'You're all settled in, then, and comfortable, over the way?' he asked them kindly. 'The brothers are looking after you, I hope?'

'Oh yes!' Linnet smiled at Brother Edward, causing two delightful dimples to appear in her rosy cheeks. 'Oh yes. Brother Francis has been looking after us. He's made us very welcome. I like him, he makes me laugh; he's got a lovely smile—like sunlight dancing on the water.'

Turning her head to speak to her brother, she did not see the look Brother Edward exchanged with Father Peregrine.

As Compline ended that evening, and the brothers in silence filed out of the chapel, the abbot stretched out a hand to detain his novice master.

'A word with you, Father Matthew. Have you sent Brother Francis to work in the guest house?'

Father Matthew looked surprised. 'No, Father, but Brother Clement may have done so. They are very short there just now with Father Gerard sick. No, I never send any novices to work among the guests, as you know. Such worldly contacts do them no good.'

'Is there anyone else who could go in his stead? One of the older brothers?'

'Well...' Father Matthew looked thoughtful. 'There's Brother Giles. He's usually helping Brother Mark with the bees just now, but maybe...'

'The bees?' the abbot interrupted him. 'That would do admirably. Brother Giles can go and help out in the guest house, and Brother Francis can help Brother Mark with his bees.'

Father Matthew looked doubtful. 'Brother Mark is very particular about his bees, Father. He won't let any of the novices but Brother Cormac near them normally. He says the others don't know how to talk to them. Brother Cormac can handle them bare-handed and without veiling his face. They like him, but the others get stung.'

'Send Brother Francis to help with the bees,' said the abbot firmly. 'It would be no bad thing to have his glory veiled for a few days. If Brother Mark has any objections he can bring them to me.'

So after their studies in the novitiate the next morning, Brother Francis walked along as far as the vegetable garden with Brother Tom. Tom worked in the vegetable patch, which lay between the abbey buildings and the orchard. The orchard was the bees' kingdom.

The bees?' said Tom in surprise. 'Brother Mark won't want you near his bees.'

'No, I know,' Francis replied. 'I don't understand it either. It was only yesterday they sent me down to the guest house, and I was enjoying that. There's a beautiful girl staying there. She took quite a shine to me, too.'

There was a silence. 'What's her name?' asked Brother Tom casually.

'Linnet. She—oh, *no*, Tom. No! Put it out of your mind. There now, go and recite the psalms at the cabbages and forget I said it.'

Tom grinned at him. 'Try your charms on the bees, then.

Brother Cormac said to tell you they like the 23rd Psalm and Gaelic love-songs.' He went in to the great sun-trap where the vegetables grew, protected from the wind on three sides by stone walls, and on the fourth by the lavender hedge which grew alongside the path to the infirmary. 'Linnet,' he murmured to himself, 'that's a pretty name. Heigh-ho. Those were the days.'

'Ah Brother, there you are.' Brother Paulinus came hobbling up the path, elderly and arthritic, a small, tough, sinewy man, whose brown eyes were bright in his weathered face. A gnome. No, a robin, thought Tom.

'Brother, we've a party of guests in the guest house, and that means horses! Would you take the handcart down to the stables and see what they've got for us, please? I want some muck for my vegetables before Brother Fidelis has it all for his roses. Bring it down this way when you return and I'll show you where to make the new heap. There's a good lad.'

Five minutes later, Brother Tom stood in the stable doorway entranced by the sight of the loveliest girl he'd ever seen crooning a song to her lame horse, stroking its ears, playing with its mane.

'By all that's holy,' he breathed, 'I never thought I'd wish I was a horse'

'Oh! Brother, you made me jump!' Linnet looked at him. 'What did you say?'

Tom shook his head and smiled at her. 'Saying my prayers,' he said. There was a pause and Linnet shyly dropped her gaze.

'My horse is lame,' she said. 'She caught her foot in a rabbit hole on the moor. It hurts her, I think.'

'Let me have a look,' said Tom. 'I used to care for the horses on the farm where I was brought up. Oh, yes, they've poulticed it and bound it right. Not too bad a sprain, I should think, but it's swollen and I expect it...' he looked up at her, '... aches.'

He released the horse's leg. 'Have you come from far?'

'We were returning to Chester. We've been visiting with my auntie. It's a shame Blanchefleur went lame, but I'm glad we came here. Everyone's been so kind and friendly. Mother says I'll have to ride pillion with Father and leave Blanchefleur here if she's not fit to ride in a day or two. Uncle would come for her, and keep her till he comes down our way. What do you think?'

'Two days?' said Tom. 'Two days? I should ask your mother to make it three. We might well have got somewhere by then. Two days seems a very short time.'

He looked at her over the mare's back, his fingers absently fondling the coarse hair of her mane, when Linnet's hand caressing the beast's neck touched his hand. The contact went through Tom's whole body like an electric shock. They both withdrew their hands. Linnet blushed, and Tom stepped backwards.

'I should go,' he said. 'I should go. I ought to be doing my work.'

'Where do you work?' Linnet enquired with a smile, dimpling her cheeks enchantingly, looking up at him through the sweep of black lashes that fringed her dewy-bright eyes.

Tom stared at her. 'I work...' he said slowly, 'in the vegetable garden.' Inside his heart was saying, Yes, oh yes, come and find me. I cannot come to you, come and find me. Forgive me, God, I haven't promised for life. Not yet. No, but I've taken my first vows. I shouldn't be doing this. Forgive me, my God. Oh, but you're beautiful.

'Brother Thomas!' Brother Paulinus' voice was calling from the stable-yard. 'Brother Thomas! Have you not got that muck loaded yet?'

'Coming!' Tom called over his shoulder. He looked back at Linnet. He tried to smile, but couldn't. 'Goodbye,' he whispered. 'Three days. If you can. For the mare.'

'Goodbye, Brother Thomas,' she smiled.

And he was gone.

✠   ✠   ✠

56

Two weeks later, Father Matthew came in great agitation to the abbot's house.

'Father, Brother Thomas has gone.'

'Gone? Where?'

'Left us. He was not at Matins, nor Lauds, nor first Mass. His bed was not slept in. He has gone. Nobody knows where he is.'

'Where is Brother Francis?'

'Brother Francis? In the scriptorium, I think. Brother Mark wouldn't keep him with the bees once he could have Brother Denis back.'

'Send him to me.'

'Father, I've asked all the novices; none of them have any idea—'

'Send him to me.'

When Francis stood before him, Father Peregrine asked him bluntly. 'What's happened?'

'Father, I can't be sure,' said Francis cautiously, but the fierce hawk's gaze gripped him.

'Don't give me that. You know him like your own self, Brother,' said Peregrine. 'What's happened?'

'Well, he said nothing to me, but... the guests who were here last week, with the lame horse... the young lady. I think he... well, he fell in love with her.'

In the silence that followed, Francis shifted uneasily.

'And how did he come to meet the young lady?' Peregrine asked him quietly.

'He met her in the stable, with the horse. Brother Paulinus sent him to the stable.' There was another moment's silence.

'So why is that troubling you?' asked Peregrine.

Francis flushed. 'I... I also told him about her. I told him her name. It was indiscreet of me, and foolish. I may already have sowed the seed in his mind. I never thought—I'm sorry.'

The abbot nodded. 'There are reasons for silence. Hardly ever has a man regretted his silence, but there are thousands who have regretted their words. Still, it can't be helped. He said nothing to you, then, about going?'

'Nothing, Father. I don't think he meant to go. I think he just couldn't bear it.'

Peregrine sighed. 'So be it. Thank you.'

Later in the week. Brother Tom's mother came up to the abbey from the nearby farm where his family lived, to return his black tunic, the habit of the order. He had called in to his family to beg some clothes and food, and to borrow some money and a horse. He would tell them nothing, but asked them to return his tunic to the abbey. She was sorry.

✠　　✠　　✠

The summer slipped away, and Tom did not return. Autumn came and went, its fogs and chills deepening into the harder cold of winter. November... December... and Tom had been gone four months. The brethren for the most part had ceased to wonder about him.

December 10th, and a bitter cold night; the ringing of the night bell to wake the brothers for the midnight Office shattered the frozen, starry skies like splinters of ice.

Abbot Peregrine's eyes opened, and he lay for a moment in the warmth of his bed, gathering the courage to brave the frosty night. He lay there a moment too long, and his eyes began to drowse shut, his body longing with a deep, sensual craving to slide blissfully back into the depths of sleep. Sleep... .

He was pulled back to wakefulness by his personal attendant, bending over him, shaking his shoulder. Peregrine levered himself up on his elbow, and swung his legs out of bed. He fumbled to put his habit on, and after a moment said in exasperation, 'I'm sorry, Brother, I need your help. My hands are as much use to me as lumps of wood in this cold.'

The young brother helped him to put on his tunic and cowl

over his under-shirt, buckled his belt for him, then knelt to fasten on his feet the night-boots of soft leather.

Stiffly, Peregrine smiled his thanks, and he reached down for the wooden crutch which lay at the side of the bed. Together they went out into the cloister and along to the huge abbey church, floodlit by the silent white moon in the frozen sky.

Father Chad joined Father Peregrine at the door of the choir, and they waited there in silence while the brothers shuffled past in file, led by Brother Stephen carrying the lantern. The last brother passed in before them and Brother Basil ceased tolling the bell. Then Father Chad and Father Peregrine followed into the choir and took their places. Abbot Peregrine gave the knock with his ring on the wood of his stall, and the community rose and began the triple-prayer and the psalms. The day had begun.

The brothers appointed to read stumbled over the words, their lips stiff with cold as well as sleepiness. Brother Theodore, giving the candle into Brother Cormac's hand as he came up to the lectern to read the fourth lesson, dripped hot tallow onto his thumb, and Brother Cormac swore, softly but audibly, causing Father Matthew to glance at him furiously. Brother Cormac was too sleepy to see or care. Father Peregrine watched his face as he returned to his stall from the lectern. It was wooden with weariness and cold, the piercing blue eyes dull with sleep. Brother Stephen, walking the rounds of the brothers with the lantern, stopped by Brother Thaddeus, who had dozed off to sleep, held the lantern in front of his eyes and shook him awake. Thaddeus took the lantern from him, as the custom was, and took his turn to carry it, treading slowly round the choir, watching that the brothers kept awake.

It was not easy, Peregrine reflected, that first year of monastic life. The young men came to the point of despair and defeat, not once, but many times, as they learned the endurance and humility that was required of them even when every nerve was at screaming pitch, suffering from cold and hunger and tiredness, from strict discipline and the rigours of penance and prayer. Not easy to turn their backs on despair and renew determination again and again, learning to continue in patience and peace, to offer all the trials up as a prayer. It never surprised him when a young man gave up on the life, came to the end of his stamina. But Brother Thomas... Brother Thomas had had a vocation, the abbot was sure of that. He wondered what had become of him.

Matins ended, and the brothers had ten minutes to stretch their legs in the cloister if they wished, while the bell tolled for Lauds. The abbot crossed the choir to where Brother Andrew remained in his stall, telling his beads as he waited for the Office to begin.

Peregrine bent down to speak quietly in his ear. 'Brother, will you serve the brethren a bowl of hot gruel each with their bread, when they break their fast? It is so bitter cold. Some of these men look in need of a little comfort. You may be excused from Prime to prepare it.'

'Aye, Father, it'll be no trouble,' the old Scotsman replied, and the abbot returned to his stall as the brothers came back in silence to their places, the cowled figures slipping like shadows among shadows in the dim and uncertain light of the candles and the lantern.

When Lauds was over, the community went back to bed for the few hours left until daybreak and the Office of Prime.

'It's insane,' grumbled Brother Cormac to Brother Francis, breaking the rule of silence as they crossed the cloister to wash themselves and comb their hair after Prime. 'It's barbaric. Is heaven offended if a man has a good night's sleep before he prays? There's not an inch of my flesh that doesn't groan in protest when that infernal bell breaks in on my sleep. It's no help to go creeping back after Lauds and shiver till morning either. It...'

'Brother Cormac,' Father Matthew's whisper reproved him, 'you have no leave for conversation.'

Cormac knelt before his novice master, saying more irritably than penitently, 'I humbly confess my fault of talking when I should be in silence, and I ask forgiveness, Father, of God and of you.'

He rose to his feet as Father Matthew blessed him. The novice master continued on his way across the cloister.

'The whole place should be towed out to sea and sunk,' muttered Brother Cormac in Brother Francis' ear. 'The only one of us who had any wits was Brother Thomas.'

Francis smiled at him and nodded; there was nothing to do with Cormac but humour him first thing on a winter's morning. Francis wondered about Tom. He missed him. He was never mentioned. They never mentioned anyone who left; but Francis had never ceased to pray for him.

Father Peregrine also had continued to pray for Brother Tom. His thoughts were on him that evening as he sat in his house after Vespers, peering over his work in the candlelight, huddled in his cloak. The room was barely warmed by the meagre fire that glowed in the hearth.

He looked up and called out '*Benedicite*!' in response to the hesitant knock at his door; and Tom came in, and stood before him. His body was tense and his face grey with cold and weariness. There was a shadow in his eyes that was new.

The abbot looked at him, and observed the pinched look that came from cold and tiredness. He also read and understood the shadow in Tom's eyes. Disillusionment. Heartache. Sorrow. He'd seen it often enough in this room.

He met Tom's gaze steadily, and in the quietness between them a little of the tension eased out of the young man.

Tom bit his lip. He stepped forward, and his hands gripped the edge of the great oak table. 'Can I come home?' he asked huskily, into the silence.

'Sit down,' said Peregrine, 'and tell me about it. I've waited for you long enough.'

Outside, the first drifting feathers of snow began to fall. Tom sat down wearily on the stool by the abbot's table. He had a long ride behind him, and a fair walk up from his parents' farm, whence he had come on foot after he had returned their horse.

'I've broken my vows,' he said sadly.

'Did you find your Linnet?'

Tom nodded. 'Linnet, little bird; yes I found her. It was a long ride and then a long search, but I found her.' He sat with his head bowed, utterly dejected, until the room seemed to fill with his hopelessness.

'Would she not have you?' Peregrine asked him gently, at last.

'Oh, yes. Yes. She… I think she loved me. Her family made me welcome. I was with them for two months. Yes, she would have had me.' His words came slowly, and so quietly, Peregrine had to strain to hear him.

'It was like a dream. It was a dream. Linnet, little bird. Such brightness… such sweetness. And she would have had me.'

'Then… ?' Father Peregrine was puzzled. Tom raised his head and looked at him out of his despair.

'I *promised*,' he said. 'The brethren and the Lord Jesus, and you. I had made my first vows. Father, I am a monk. How could I stand before God and vow myself Linnet's man, when I am already vowed to holy poverty, holy obedience… holy chastity? I mustn't… mustn't break my promise.'

'Did you tell Linnet this?'

Tom nodded miserably.

'And you really want to come back to us? Is it that you feel constrained by your vows or is it a thing of your heart?'

'Father, this is my home. This is my life. There is nowhere else for me. This is where my peace is. Will you have me back?'

Peregrine considered the young man before him. 'It is a grave thing you have done,' he said at length. 'The brethren will need some convincing. For myself… .' His grey eyes searched Tom's. 'God knows, we all stumble, we all fall. One thing I must ask, take it not amiss. Linnet: you are sure you have not left her with child?'

Tom shook his head. 'No. I did not—we did not—no. She could not be with child.'

Father Peregrine weighed it in his mind one more moment,

then stooped down and gathered up his wooden crutch. 'Come to the kitchen, then,' he said as he pushed back his chair and stood up. 'You look hungry and bone-weary. Eat well, and sleep here in my house tonight. Tomorrow you must begin again, asking to be admitted here. I cannot promise the brothers will have you back, but I will do what I can. If they will receive you, it hardly needs me to tell you there would be room for no more such mistakes. Come now, eat heartily and sleep well. We will see what tomorrow brings.'

✠   ✠   ✠

The ritual of begging admittance to the abbey was almost, but not quite, a formality. The aspirant had to stand outside the great gates of the abbey and beat on them with his fist. The man in question would, of course, have been to see the abbot long before, and be expected in the community. The form was that the abbot and his prior would open the gate to him, with the question, 'What do you ask of us?' The man at the gate would then ask, according to the custom of the abbey, 'I beg you for the love of God to admit me to this house, that I may do penance, amend my life and serve God faithfully until death,' and the abbot would welcome him in. There were occasions though—and this was one of them—when the community had reason to be unsure of the man begging admittance at the gate. They then tested the sincerity of his intentions by the simple but surprisingly effective method of keeping him waiting.

The morning after his arrival back at the abbey, Tom was still sleeping off the exhaustion that followed weeks of troubled nights and conflicting emotions, while Father Peregrine was addressing the community Chapter meeting.

'Brother Thomas has returned to us,' he said, and took note of the guarded expressions, the slightly pursed lips of some men, the surprise and interest of others.

'I cannot, under the circumstances, take it upon myself to admit him here again without the goodwill of the community. I have talked with him, and I will vouch for him that he comes with a pure intention, burdened with no mortal sin. He is wiser by his experience, and truly sorry for his conduct. In my judgement, his return to us is the action of a man submitting to a true call of God. Brothers, I beseech you; be merciful. Think on your own weakness, and be not over-hasty to condemn. You have today and tomorrow and the next day to pray and consider. The day after that I will take counsel of you and we will come to a decision. I ask only this: that you seek God's wisdom and you search your own heart; but let no man presume to discuss the matter with his brother except at the Chapter meeting today or tomorrow morning. Has any of you a question to ask?'

'I have.' Old Brother Prudentius rose to his feet. 'It is true, is it not, that Brother Thomas left because of a woman?' A slight murmur rippled through the community. Peregrine, sitting imperturbably in the great abbatial chair, listened to it. Embarrassment, he detected, and disapproval. He inclined his head slightly in assent, but said nothing.

'Four months is a long time,' continued Brother Prudentius. 'Why has he come back? Has she jilted him? Is he weary of her? Why the change of heart after so long?'

'It is a long time, Brother, I agree. No, she did not abandon him, nor did he weary of her. He came back because of his promises to Almighty God. He would not make a marriage vow, having once vowed himself to serve God as a monk, in his first vows here.'

'But Father, surely he has broken his vows?'

Father Peregrine took a deep breath and let it go in a sigh. He looked down for a moment, then lifted his gaze to meet Brother Prudentius' eyes.

'And which of us has never done so? Is there a man here among us who can boast perfect poverty, perfect chastity, perfect obedience? God have mercy on me, I make no such claim. But

I have promised and therefore persevere. His was the weakness of youth and vitality. Our weakness as his pastors was that of negligence. We failed him no less than he failed us. He offers us the grace of trying again. Most good shepherds seek their lost sheep. We are lucky. Ours has returned of its own accord.'

And I couldn't really push them harder than that, Peregrine reflected as he returned to his house after Chapter, to find Brother Tom, having woken, washed, dressed and found himself some breakfast, awaiting further instruction.

'Have you eaten well?' asked Peregrine. 'Are you sure now? Then borrow my cloak, for you'll need it. You must go out of the gates and seek admittance again. Be of good courage.'

Tom walked out of the abbey, through the little postern door set in the great gate and heard it click shut behind him. He stood on the road, looking up at the turbulent sky, banked with cloud of deepening tones of grey. The wind was sharp as a knife and he wrapped Peregrine's cloak around him, glad of its protection. The snow that had fallen in the night was mostly melting, but the puddles lying in the wheel-ruts and pot-holes of the road were frozen over.

Tom thought of Linnet, the last sight he had of her, standing very still, silent tears rolling down her cheeks, her eyes drinking in everything about him and storing it away in her heart. The dreariness and hostility of the weather suited his mood as he turned again to face the great door, asking himself, 'Am I really going to do this?' Then he raised his hand, clenched hard into a fist, and beat on the abbey gate. There was no response. He raised his fist again, and thundered on the massive door. There was still no response. Tom stood, nonplussed, for a moment, then remembered Father Peregrine's words, 'Have you eaten well? Are you sure now? Then borrow my cloak, for you'll need it,' and he understood. They meant to make him wait.

He wandered about a bit, leaned on the wall and gazed out across the valley, looked down the road towards the village, watched the rooks squabbling in the trees at the roadside. He bent down and picked up a little stick that lay on the road, peeled the bark off it, broke it into bits and threw the pieces away, one by one. The wind was stinging his ears, and he covered them with his hands, but that left his cloak flapping free, so he wrapped it about him again. How long does this go on for? he wondered.

He went again and beat on the door, but no one came. Feeling slightly foolish, he turned away and sauntered about. He tried to whistle a tune, but the wind snatched the breath from his lips. 'Mother of God, it's cold,' he muttered, and moved close to the shelter of the abbey wall.

After a while a cart came up the road on business at the abbey. The carter stopped at the gate, glanced at Tom in curiosity, then went through the postern to seek admittance from Brother Cyprian, the porter. The great gate swung open, and the man came out and led his horse through. The cartwheels rumbled across the flags of the yard and the horse's hooves clattered loud on the stone. Brother Cyprian, closing the gate, nodded to Tom standing there, but had neither word nor smile for him. The noise of the gate as it clanged shut leaving Tom outside echoed through his head, his heart, his soul. He thought of his mother and father. They would be at home now, eating a hearty meal before a roaring fire. And Linnet? Baking maybe, or sitting with her mother and little sister at the hearthside, spinning or sewing. He wondered if she thought of him too. In the abbey now, the midday Office and meal would be over, the brethren going quietly about their work. Francis would be blowing a little warmth back into his numb fingers in the scriptorium. He would be through with that Book of Psalms now. Tom wondered how much of the illumination of it Brother Francis had accomplished himself, and how much Brother Clement had rejected in favour of Brother Theodore's superior artistry. He could imagine Brother Clement's face, frowning in irritation as he perused the book, the mediocre lettering, the uneven quality of the illumination divided between Brother Theodore's and Brother

Francis' efforts, the parchment grubby with sweat and worn with too much erasing. The months of work would likely be dismissed with dry disfavour—'I doubt if this is one for posterity, Brother.' Fortunately Francis was used to it, and his good humour was equal to it. It would be good to see Francis again. Tom was not a solitary man. He liked company and conversation; he liked to work alongside other men. The loneliness outside the abbey seemed as final and chilling as hell. The leaden despair of it took hold of him and filled him. 'Sing something,' he said to himself. 'What shall I sing? A psalm, anything.'

He began to sing, and the words that came to his lips were the words of the Misere: '*Misere mei Deus, secundum magnam misericordiam tuam. Et secundum multitudinem miserationum tuarum, dele iniquitatem meam.* Have mercy on me, O God, after thy great goodness: according to the multitude of thy mercies, do away mine offences.'

As he sang the mournful chant, sorrow welled up in him, and though the words came of their own accord to his tongue, his mind was not on them. I've broken my vows, disgraced myself, and they may never have me back, he thought. Oh, if they won't have me, what then?

'*Cor mundum crea in me Deus: et spiritum rectum innova in visceribus meis. Ne projicias me a facie tua: et spiritum sanctum tuum ne auferas a me.* Make me a clean heart, O God: and renew a right spirit within me. Cast me not away from your presence and take not your holy spirit from me.'

His throat ached with forlorn misery, and he abandoned the chant.

The heavy catch of the gate was lifted from within with a clang, and Tom turned towards it, hopeful. But it was only the farmer, bringing his horse and cart home. Tom turned his face away, sick at heart. He would not look at the farmer, though he felt the man's eyes on him. They were not well acquainted, but they knew each other, and Tom had no wish to submit to his questions, or his banter. The abbey gate swung shut and the cart was on its way. The gloomy day began to darken with the shadows of evening, and Tom wondered what time it was. Three o'clock maybe. Half past. The woollen cloak was no longer much protection against the cold. Desperately he beat again on the door, then stood humiliated in the indifferent silence.

It was getting really dark now. Brother Stephen would be bringing the cows in for milking, and soon it would be time for Vespers.

'Faith, I'm hungry,' Tom muttered to himself. 'I could even face Cormac's bread and count it a blessing.'

The bell rang for Vespers. Faintly, intermittently, he heard snatches of the brothers singing the Office in the abbey church in the moments when the wind dropped. It was completely dark now, but there were no stars visible. They were all hidden behind the mass of clouds.

Tom looked up at the great looming bulk of the abbey that towered beside him. I've been here *hours*, he thought. He hesitated a moment, then stepped swiftly to the door and raised his fist, hammering and hammering on the rough, wet wood. The thunder of his knocking echoed in the black silence. There was no response.

The postern door set in the gate opened presently, and one or two of the villagers who worked in the abbey came out, returning home to their families. Tom drew back into the shadow of the wall, unwilling to be discovered by the light of their lantern. He heard Brother Cyprian's cheery 'God give you goodnight!' and was seized by the most abject, engulfing self-pity that he had ever known. He sank down onto his haunches, squatting on his heels, huddled into his cloak in the scant protection from the wind that the abbey wall offered. 'Oh, come *on*,' he groaned aloud. He had never been so cold and hungry and tired in his life. He seemed to have fallen into a pit of icy black timelessness.

The bell rang for Compline, and again he heard distant drifts of chanting. After that, the utter profound stillness of the Great

Silence descended on the abbey, and a new thought spread like a dark stain of incredulous horror through Tom's soul. Oh God, they're not going to leave me here all *night*?

It was then that it started to snow.

Tom looked up at the sky, and the snowflakes settled on his eyelashes, melted in his eyebrows, settled softly onto his face, little dreary kisses of cold wetness. He hunched his shoulders, wrapped his arms about himself, shivering, and bent his face down into his body warmth. Crouched thus in the corner of the gateway to glean what pitiful shelter he could, Tom passed the night dozing fitfully. The cold seemed to have seeped through to his bones and hunger gnawed at him mercilessly. He clung to the hope of the morning when the gate would open, 'What do you ask of us?' and the nightmare would be over. He fell asleep towards dawn, but was woken by the sound of voices. Two of the villagers who worked in the kitchens were coming along the road. Tom shrank back against the wall, drawing into the blackness of his cloak, and was thankful to escape the men's notice as they passed through the inset door.

The Office bell began to ring. The snow had ceased for the time being, but the air was still and the sky hung heavy with cloud. The occasional snowflake drifted down. Tom rose stiffly to his feet and stamped about a bit, clapping his arms against his sides. The pain of the cold in his feet, especially his toes, was acute, and his ears ached in the wind.

After a time he heard the door of the porter's lodge as Brother Cyprian came back from first Mass. The sun rose, its first faint flush of pink swelling to a crescendo of crimson glory in the east. The blush of beauty faded as the day wore on, hour after hour, until the sun was suspended, a white remote ball of light in a leaden sky.

Straggles of the faithful trudged up from the village to the abbey church for ten o'clock Mass after Chapter, and Tom kept out of sight as best he could. He watched them return again down the hill, bundled in shawls, wearing stockings over their clogs so as not to slip on the icy roads. His eyes followed them until they turned the bend in the road and were lost to view, and then he watched the rooks squabbling in their high, precarious nests, listened to their disconsolate cawing. He looked down at the puddles in the pot-holes, white where air was trapped under the ice, and grey where water touched the frozen surface. One or two blades of grass poked through the flatness of the ice. Far away a dog yelped, its cry carrying in the cold, and a blackbird cackled in alarm in the hedgerow at the top of the road. Into the hopeless eternity of the day, the abbey bell tolled for the midday Office. The sun hung overhead, its glory contracted to a wintry sphere of severity.

Through the afternoon, Tom either squatted in the corner of the gateway, leaning against the wall, or else he walked to and fro, beating his arms about his ribs to try and keep warm. Sometimes he whispered the words of the prayers the brothers would be saying in the chapel. He thought back over all that had happened in the last few months, remembered that first casual conversation with Francis, standing in the summer garden—What's her name? Linnet—oh no, Tom, put it out of your mind… It seemed a lifetime ago. Even his thoughts ran sluggishly, frozen. He felt as though he'd been there forever. Once or twice he beat with his fist on the door, but less often, and with less conviction.

A few callers came and went. Tom bent his head and would not meet their inquisitive gaze. Then the sun was sinking again in a wide glow of ochre light. Darkness, and the Vespers bell, and he sank down hopelessly and sat with his arms tightly round his knees, his head resting on the top of his knees, trying to conserve what vestige of warmth he had. His head ached with hunger and he was thirsty too. After a while he stretched out his hand and scooped up some of the snow that had drifted against the wall, and ate it. He satisfied his thirst with snow, and felt the coldness penetrate inside him.

The Compline bell rang, and then came the deep silence of the night. 'No…' Tom whispered to himself. 'No, not another night. Oh, please, no.'

By the middle of that night, Tom could no longer distinguish between the ache of the cold, the ache of hunger and the aching of his cramped body. It snowed again in the night, a light, persistent snowfall, and he felt the dampness oozing through the thick woollen cloak.

In the early hours of the morning, he stood up clumsily to stretch his cramped and aching limbs.

I've had enough, he thought dully. I'm going home. He trudged fifty yards down the road, then stopped. What if they opened the gate now, after all this waiting, and found him gone? He turned back, running and stumbling up the road to the silent black mountain of the abbey. 'This is my home,' he said aloud.

But what if they never open the door to me? he thought. He searched his memory, trying to think if he had ever heard of anyone who had not even been rejected, but simply ignored, left outside, forgotten. In the lightening grey of the dawn, he sat down again on the abbey threshold and resumed his weary, aching vigil. Just before sunrise, he heard the click of the postern door, and scrambled to his feet, wild with hope. It was old Brother Andrew from the kitchen. 'I've permission to bring you this,' he said. He held in his hands a steaming bowl of soup. Torn between bitter disappointment and abject gratitude, Tom reached out his hands without a word. He drank the soup greedily, spilling some, his hands and mouth clumsy with cold.

'Thank you,' he said, as he held the empty bowl out to Brother Andrew, 'that was grand. I thought maybe you'd all forgotten me,' he added with an attempt at a smile.

Brother Andrew shook his head. 'No, lad,' he said, 'we've not forgotten you.' Then he took the bowl and went back inside. Tom resisted the temptation to beg him to wait, to come back. Oh God, would it never end? It was like a bad dream.

That day he sat, most of the day, motionless against the wall, no longer bothering to hide from those who came and went, colder than he had ever thought it was possible to be. The wind

71

cut through to his marrow. He felt bone-cold, as cold as stone. He couldn't imagine ever being warm again and he tortured himself, conjuring up memories of the blaze of logs in the warming room fireplace. His head ached in a constant dull throb, and he shivered in his damp clothes.

Evening came, and nightfall and again the snow, and still they left him there. By morning he lay on his side in the snow on the threshold against the abbey gate, shuddering with cold and fever, numb and half-delirious, simply enduring.

✠　✠　✠

Inside the abbey, as the community was gathering for Chapter, the abbot with his prior, Father Chad, and his infirmarian, Brother Edward, went and opened the great gate. Tom looked up at them, and raised himself on his hands, awkwardly, until he knelt, after a fashion, at the abbot's feet. Through the dizzy waves of fever that clouded his head he heard Father Peregrine saying to him, 'What do you ask of us, my son?' and that firm warm voice spoke hearth and home to him, journey's end.

'For... the... love... of... God...' Tom's lips felt like slabs of clay, robbed of all feeling. 'For... the... love of God... Father... I can't say... it. No... admit... me... .' He looked up at Father Peregrine and was overwhelmed by the blaze of love and compassion that met him there.

'Help him,' said Peregrine abruptly. 'Father Chad, Brother Edward, help him to his feet.'

'Father, he's in a bad way. He's burning up with fever and his clothes are sodden. Should we not take him straight to the infirmary?'

'No,' said the abbot. 'Bring him to Chapter.'

Father Chad and Brother Edward half-supported, half-carried Tom to the Chapter House, where the community was gathered.

The abbot took his seat in the great carved chair and looked at

Tom as he stood, held up by the infirmarian and the prior.

'Thank you, brothers. Let him stand alone,' he said.

'But, Father...' protested Father Chad.

'Let him stand alone,' repeated the abbot. Father Chad, Brother Edward, go to your places.'

As they left him, Tom swayed on his feet for a moment, his teeth chattering and his body shivering uncontrollably, the room swimming before his eyes. Then his legs gave way under him and he fell on his hands and knees to the floor.

'What do you ask of this community, my son?' the abbot asked him calmly.

'I beg of you... for the love of God...' the words came slow and slurred, 'to forgive me... and admit me again... to this house... here to do penance... amend my... life... and serve God... faithfully... until death...'

Tom tried to raise his head, but it felt like a lead weight. He knelt on the floor, his arms, which were shaking with fever and fatigue, braced to prevent him from collapsing altogether.

'I think under the circumstances, brothers, it would be unreasonable to ask this man to go and wait outside while the community votes.' The abbot's voice was aloof and dispassionate. He paused, allowing them to listen for a moment to the shuddering, almost sobbing, labour of Tom's breathing.

'I ask of you, brothers, will you have him back? Those in favour, please raise your hands... and those against... thank you. My son, we welcome you into this house. May God grant you grace so to amend your life, to do penance and serve him faithfully until death, as you have requested. *Deo gratias.* Brother Edward, Brother John, get him to bed.'

☒ ☒ ☒

Floating in a light-headed haze of fever, Tom submitted gratefully to the care of Brother Edward and Brother John in the infirmary.

73

They stripped him of his wet clothes and rubbed him dry. They gently chafed the feeling back into his hands and feet as he sat wrapped in a blanket before a glowing fire of sweet-smelling apple logs. They dosed him with infusions of elderflower and peppermint, and gave him warm milk and honey to drink.

'I know you're hungry, lad, but it's no good you trying to eat in this state. Just take this for now, then a good sleep and we'll see.'

They warmed a shirt for him by the fire and dressed him in it, and tucked him into bed like a child, having washed his hands and face and combed his hair. There was a hot brick wrapped in cloths at his feet, and one at his back, and Tom lay in a peaceful daze, contentedly smelling the lavender of the infirmary sheets as he sank into the blissful relief of sleep.

'I think he'll be all right in a day or two,' said Brother Edward quietly to Brother John. 'His chest is clear at the moment. Keep him warm and watch him, and don't let him eat too much too soon. God bless him, he's a brave lad. We'll let him sleep now. That's the best thing for him.'

They went softly from the room and closed the door. Brother John stood with his arms full of Tom's wet clothes, his face troubled.

'That was a heartless way to treat him, Brother. I don't understand it. To have him kneel before us all—poor soul, it was cruel.'

Brother Edward chuckled. 'Come and dump his wet things in a pail before you're soaked yourself—and treat them with respect. That's Father Abbot's good winter cloak you have there, if I'm not mistaken. Heartless, you think? Don't you believe it, Brother. Father Abbot would give his life for that lad. You just wait and see who comes and sits at his bedside as he sweats out his fever through the night. How were you intending to vote when you came to Chapter?'

'I wasn't sure. It was a serious thing he'd done. I don't know even now—but seeing him kneeling there—poor soul, what he'd been through! I'd not the heart to vote against him. It could have killed him, three nights in that bitter weather.'

'Not him, Brother John, he's as strong as an ox. It would take more than an east wind and a fall of snow to snuff that lad out.'

'Aye, maybe, but it was hard-hearted. Father showed him no pity at all.'

Edward shook his head, smiling. 'No, no, that's not the way it is. Brother Thomas has a welcome in this house again and it would have taken nothing less to win it for him. He's a man in a thousand is our abbot, Brother John. He knows what he's about. And he holds this community in the palm of his hand.'

☩   ☩   ☩

I lay on my front in the grass, absentmindedly pulling apart a daisy, watching the seagulls wheeling over the harbour. There was a fishing boat out at sea on its own. All the others were drawn up on the shingle at this time of day.

'I like Brother Tom,' I said. 'That was a good story.'

'Yes, it was one of my favourites when I was your age. But I liked Father Peregrine best. It's a skilled job, that,' Mother said thoughtfully, looking out at the solitary fishing boat coming in towards the beach, 'bringing a boat safely into harbour. Especially on stormy nights when the sea is rough.'

She yawned and stretched her arms above her head.

'It's a good story, but a long one. I could sit here all day, but I expect they'll be wondering at home where we are, and wanting their tea. Let's go back.'

'When you began,' I said, linking my arm in Mother's as we started down the lane home, 'I thought it was going to be a story about Brother Francis. It started off about him.'

'Francis? Yes. He and Brother Tom tend to turn up in the same places. Although actually Brother Francis' story is quite different from that, at least, in some ways. He had his struggles too, but they were different from Tom's.'

'Will you tell me Brother Francis' story? Will you tell me it tonight?'

Mother laughed. 'Not tonight, no. I've had enough storytelling for one day, and I've promised Mary I'll read a whole chapter of *The Wind in the Willows* before bed. Tomorrow, maybe.'

'Tomorrow,' I said firmly, 'for sure.'

CHAPTER FOUR

The Poor in Spirit

Cecily had put something up her nose. She came running in to Mother from the garden with an air of great importance, to communicate her news.

'There is a stone inside my nose,' she said impressively.

'Oh, no! Let me look. Come here, into the light by the window. Oh heavens, there is too. Just a minute, let me get my tweezers.'

Mother went for the tweezers that she kept hidden away in her box of private things. She would never let the little ones play with them, because she said some pairs of tweezers were better than others, and having in the past wasted her money on tweezers that wouldn't work properly, she didn't want to lose a good pair. She kept them for plucking out the bristly hairs that grew on her chin. In general Mother was in favour of hair, and refused to shave the hair off her legs or under her arms like Therese and I did. But then she wouldn't go swimming at the sports centre because she was embarrassed to be the only lady with hairy legs and armpits. She didn't mind the beach, because you can get away from people there. So what she thought about it wasn't quite straightforward. As she said herself, you can't always close the gap between what is and what ought to be. Anyway, she drew the line at bristly chins.

She poked about in Cecily's nose with the tweezers, but the stone, though it was low enough to be seen, was too high up and too well-lodged to be freed with the tweezers.

'I daren't push it at all in case it goes even further. Beth, fetch me the pepper. Honestly, Cecily, you really are the end.'

Beth brought the pepper and Mother shook some onto the back of her hand.

'Here, sniff this,' she said, holding it up to Cecily's nose. Cecily obediently sniffed it, and sniffed it some more. Her eyes watered a bit, but nothing else happened.

'Oh dear. Bother it. I'd better phone your daddy. He'd be coming home in half an hour anyway. We'll have to take you to the hospital.'

Mother phoned Daddy at the book-binding place where he worked, and he said he would come home straight away and take them in the car up to the hospital.

'Therese, will you give Mary and Beth their tea if I'm not back in an hour?' said Mother. 'You can heat up the stew from yesterday, and there's an apple pie in the cupboard. Open a tin of evaporated milk. I don't know when we'll be home. You know what it's like waiting in Casualty. You could grow old and die before you ever saw a doctor. Come on, Cecily, don't start crying. You'll be all right. Fetch a book to look at and a dolly to play with.'

'Can I come too?' I asked.

'We'll be a long time, Melissa. Are you sure?'

'Yes, I can bring my homework.'

I wanted to see what the doctor would do.

Daddy came home, and we bundled Cecily, who was whimpering by now, into the car, and set off for the hospital, leaving Mary and Beth waving in the doorway.

The hospital was a large, dingy building constructed of flat expanses of pale blue stuff and plate-glass windows. There were no spaces left in the car park, so Daddy went in search of somewhere to park while Mother and I took Cecily in.

Cecily and I sat on two of the chairs that lined the corridor while Mother gave our details to the receptionist who sat behind a glass panel in the wall.

A wide doorway led out of our corridor into the next corridor. That was also lined with chairs and people sitting on them, waiting. A notice over the doorway said 'X-RAY' with an arrow pointing one way and 'FRACTURES' with an arrow pointing the other way. The walls were painted with buff-coloured gloss paint. Under the plate-glass window that looked out onto the car park stood an old-fashioned radiator, and in front of it a low coffee table stacked with back copies of *Country Life*. Someone had pushed a cardboard box with some rather dirty toys in it half under the table. On the wall opposite me stood a fish tank. There was coloured gravel in the bottom of it, out of which grew two pieces of water weed. I counted the tropical fish swimming among the weed. I could not be sure because they were very small and kept disappearing from view, but I think there were about five.

Mother came and sat down beside us. 'I do hope we won't be here too long,' she said. 'Come and sit on my knee, Cecily. I'll read you your book.'

Cecily shook her head. 'It hurts in my nose,' she said. 'I want the stone out now.'

A doctor (I suppose he was a doctor; he was wearing a white coat with the buttons undone) came walking along our corridor, out into the next corridor where the other people were sitting. He stopped beside a rather prissy-looking lady with a little girl, about five years old. The little girl's arm was encased in a plaster.

The doctor looked down at the little girl. 'Hello,' he said, in a jolly sort of way, 'how are you?' The little girl stared at him, and didn't say anything. The doctor had short, frizzy black hair except for a bald bit on top. He was wearing glasses with gold rims. He kept his hands in his pockets, and he had a clipboard tucked under his left arm. He smiled at the little girl, but she didn't smile back. He took his hand out of his pocket, and took hold of the clipboard and read the papers on the front of it for a minute.

'Well, Mrs er... Robbins,' he said in a brisk sort of way, looking up from the clipboard at the lady, 'this shouldn't take a moment. We'll just take her dressing off and have a look at her. All right?'

'Thank you, doctor,' murmured the lady, but the silent little girl came to life quite unexpectedly.

'No!' she cried out. 'No! You can't! No!' She sounded quite panicky. The lady with her looked embarrassed and cross. 'Don't be silly, Sarah,' she said sharply.

'Oh, don't you worry,' said the doctor. 'We'll have that dressing off in no time.'

'Stop it, Sarah. Don't be such a naughty girl.' The lady's voice was rising in irritation over the top of the little girl's voice. She was screaming incoherently, 'No! No! No! You can't take my dress off,' and starting to cry.

'Now come on, Sarah. If you'll just bring her along here, Mrs er... we'll have it off in no time,' said the doctor.

They disappeared down the corridor out of sight, the little girl still crying and protesting, her mother still telling her off.

Why didn't he listen? Why didn't he think? What was the matter with him? I looked at Mother, who was shaking her head in disbelief.

'I'll bet you that child's never heard the word "dressing" before,' she said. 'Her mother will *always* have called it a plaster. Somebody needs to tell these young men that unless you listen and observe, and use your imagination to get below the surface of what you see, you're not fit to be trusted with other people's lives. Silly fool. That was our name they called there, wasn't it?

80

Come on, Cecily. Now you must be brave, and very, very good. If you want that stone out you must do exactly as the doctor says. No crying and no fuss.'

Our doctor was a lady doctor. She had a small office in a cubicle at the edge of the ward. It had a big poster on the wall, covered in colour photographs of all the different kinds of injuries it was possible to do to your eye, and underneath each picture the information about appropriate treatment.

Mother sat down with Cecily on her knee, and I stood in the doorway, because there was no room for another person. Mother explained what Cecily had done and the doctor listened quietly.

'Can I have a look in your nose?' she asked Cecily. Cecily nodded, solemnly. She tipped back her head, with a tragic look on her face. I think she was enjoying it, really. The doctor had a pencil-shaped torch to peer into Cecily's nose.

'Oh yes, I can see it quite easily,' she said. 'Stay like that and I'll see if I can get it out.'

She had a long, fine steel instrument with a circular loop at the end, and she used this as she tried carefully to hook out the stone. All she got was a bit of snot. She sat back thoughtfully.

'Mmm...' she said. 'I'll have another go, and if that fails we shall have to try something else.'

But Cecily suddenly drew in her breath and sneezed an enormous sneeze. The little stone shot across the table and ricocheted under the doctor's desk.

'That thing tickled my nose,' she said.

When we got out into the corridor again, Daddy was sitting there, flicking through a copy of *Country Life*.

'Look, I've found the house for us,' he said. His thumb was marking a page with a picture of an old farmhouse. It had a thatched roof, and its sloping lawn ran down to a duck pond. There were big oak trees dotted about here and there in its garden. Mother smiled. 'One day,' she said.

The doctor had given Cecily her stone wrapped up in a tissue, and Cecily showed it to Daddy, and to Mary and Beth and Therese when we got home. They all admired it respectfully.

I told Daddy, in indignation, about the little girl and her plaster. He listened and nodded.

'When you grow up, Melissa, my dove,' he said, 'remember that little girl. You can go to university and train your intellect. You can go to college and learn all sorts of skills. You can be an apprentice and be taught a trade. But, understanding… you yourself must listen to the wisdom of life itself to learn understanding. They can't teach you that in university, or medical school, or technical college, or anywhere in the world. Now then, I don't know about you, but I fancy a bit of cheese on toast.'

At bedtime, Cecily's stone was put in a jam jar on the mantelpiece, and I carried her up to bed while Mother checked Mary's and Beth's teeth in the bathroom.

Mother read them a story and they played their bedtime game and had their prayers, then she tucked them into bed.

'Mother, you said you'd tell me about Brother Francis,' I said when they were snuggled in.

'Yes, I know. I haven't forgotten. Draw the curtains and light the candle. Dear me, it's been a long day. Ah, that's better. Settle down now, Cecily. Stop wriggling like that.'

✠   ✠   ✠

Well then, this is Brother Francis' story. What do you know about him? Not much, I think, except that he was Brother Tom's friend and made him laugh. The two of them had grown up together in the same neighbourhood, and they both came from farming families, but Brother Francis' family were richer, and of considerable social standing. So although they had been acquainted, it was not until the differences between them were ironed out by their shared life of simplicity and poverty in Christ's service that they discovered each other as friends. Of course, a man in monastic life was not supposed to have any particular friendships, being given as a friend to all men for love of Christ, but set apart from intimate relationships, again for love of Christ. But understanding flourished more readily between some men than others, and in that abbey natural affection was seen as a grace and a gift, provided it did not begin to develop into the kind of friendship that made other people feel shut out or unwanted. And Brother Tom and Brother Francis got on well. Any time you wanted to know how Brother Tom was, you could ask Brother Francis and he could tell you at once, because he loved him and understood him, and also because Brother Thomas was a straightforward kind of man who shouted when he was angry, wept when he was sad, and fell asleep when he was weary—whether that was in bed, or during the long psalms of the night Office, or in the middle of Father Matthew's Greek lessons.

Any time you had asked Brother Thomas how Brother Francis was, though, he would probably have said, 'All right—I think. He seems cheerful enough.' Because Francis always did. He was courteous, he studied hard, he prayed earnestly, he had a smile for everyone, and he kept his own counsel regarding his private thoughts and feelings. He was cheerful at all times, and had an irrepressible sense of humour which, along with a tendency to get into conversation at the wrong times, got him into disgrace now and then. Brother Francis made himself pleasant to everyone and was well-liked. If he had a dark side, it was not obvious. If he had troubles, no one knew; and everyone was well content with this state of affairs, except Father Matthew.

'He's like the froth on a wave, that young man,' he would say to Father Peregrine. 'There's something insubstantial about him. All this light-heartedness is pleasant enough, but he seems insincere to me. He's not a minstrel or a court jester, he's a man of prayer and he ought to behave like one. He's too happy. You mark my words, this eternal smile of his covers an emptiness within. He needs sobering up, that lad. We must be more strict with him.'

The abbot considered the matter. Father Matthew, though admittedly not the most sensitive of men in helping the novices in his care through their struggles, did have, one could not deny it, an uncanny ability to spot and expose their weaknesses. If he said Brother Francis was too happy, he probably was too happy. He was certainly getting under Father Matthew's skin.

'I'll talk to him,' Father Peregrine said finally one Wednesday evening when Father Matthew had buttonholed him on the way out of Vespers. 'I'll see him after Chapter tomorrow.'

The abbot thought about Francis as he waited for him the next day. It was a fresh, chill day in early spring, when the snowdrops were out and the jasmine growing on the wall was tentatively blossoming, but not the primroses yet. Father Peregrine liked Francis, though he did not believe Brother Francis had ever really taken him into his confidence. 'Insincere... an emptiness within... .' The abbot pondered Father Matthew's words. The judgement seemed a bit unkind and dismissive.

He recognised Brother Francis' firm, quick knock at the door, which stood ajar. The knock was like the man: confident, but not arrogant.

Father Peregrine pushed back his chair, deciding not to sit behind his great table full of books to talk to this young man. He picked up his crutch from where it lay beside him on the floor, and stood up to cross the room. Again the knock, not growing impatient, rather its assurance diminishing. The abbot hastened to the door. He kept it ajar when he was not in private conversation, partly to be welcoming, and partly because the heavy iron latch on the door was not easy for his broken hands to manipulate.

'Come in, Brother.' He smiled at Francis as he pulled the door open. 'Come and sit down over here. Are you cold? Would you like to light a fire?'

'A fire?' Brother Francis hesitated at the prospect of this unfamiliar luxury.

'Yes? The things are there at the hearth. Your hands are abler than mine; I shall fumble if I try to light it.'

The abbot settled himself into one of the two low wooden chairs that stood near the fireplace, and watched Brother Francis as he set about making the fire. His movements were deft and brisk, economical.

There were some men it was easier to talk to by the fire, who could not easily look into Peregrine's eyes and tell their troubles, but unwound as they looked into the dancing flames and relaxed in the warmth. Father Peregrine thought it might well be so with Francis.

It was a long time since Brother Francis had occasion to build a fire. Dry sticks and cones over a twist of dried grass. Some rosemary twigs cut in the summer saved for the sweet-smelling winter kindling, that catches well. Then the little apple logs, gnarled and speckled with blue lichen. An old candle stump on top of the pile to encourage it along.

Father Peregrine watched him. I like him, he thought. His bearing is composed but modest. Yes, there's no swagger to him. Alert, intelligent face and plenty of humour there. Well, he needs that, no doubt. It's not an easy life. The abbot felt a bit like Pilate, looking for a fault and finding none, saying desperately to the Jews, 'But I find nothing wrong in this man.' There was a little nervousness about him maybe, a certain tension around his shoulders and neck, and his fingernails were well bitten. Having got his little fire going, he sat back on the hearthstone and looked up at Father Peregrine. The ready smile that caused Father Matthew such foreboding flashed a bit too quickly maybe, but then... being required to discuss his vocation with his superior was unlikely to set him at his ease.

'There, you've made a better job of it than I would have. Sit for a while and enjoy the warmth now. I'll not keep you too long. Brother Clement will be missing you in the scriptorium.'

Brother Francis laughed. 'Yes, like a headache, I should think.'

'Does he dislike you? He has never complained of you.'

'It is my illumination work that is his sorest trial. "Will you look at the knowing smirk you've done on the face of Our Lady, Brother Francis," he says to me, and, "What is this monstrous being here? Is it an *angel* with this lewd wink and cunning leer? For shame, Brother, it is a holy thing you've rendered thus like a brutish yokel in a tavern, three parts drunk!"'

Peregrine was laughing in spite of himself at Brother Francis' exact mimicry of Brother Clement's refined dismay. Francis grinned at him.

'No, he bids me stick to flowers now, for flowers have no expressions to disgrace their faces. I doubt if he sighs much over my absence this morning. He must think the good Lord has given him an unexpected holiday.'

Father Peregrine shook his head. 'I must see these works of art for myself one day. I remember him speaking of a thing of the Last Judgement you had painted that went somehow amiss.'

'Oh that, yes. He had me erase it and give it to Brother Theodore to finish in the end. I thought it was coming on quite well. I'd meant to paint a scowling devil glaring over the souls of the damned, and I was thinking of Brother Cormac first thing in the morning when Father Matthew berates him for his Latin; and it was shaping quite well I thought, black-browed and a kind of ugly look in his eye, but Brother Clement didn't like it at all. "It looks like an Irish pedlar with the belly-ache!" he exclaimed, which made me smile, because I'd got it more true than I intended. "And what is this simpering Christ like a silly lass sighing for her sweetheart? Brother, no more! Your lettering is adequate, but these caricatures give me a pain," he said. Yes, that was my Last Judgement.'

He laughed and looked into the fire, pushed the little logs together and watched the sparks fly. Peregrine could see that his conversation would not be to Father Matthew's taste. 'Apart from your disasters in the scriptorium, how are you finding the life, my son?' he asked him.

Brother Francis smiled. 'When I'm not too hungry to raise my thoughts above my belly, I get a glimpse of heaven now and then.'

'You don't have enough to eat?'

'Oh, I didn't mean it really, no, no. The food here is good, and it drives us to prayer, you know—"Of your goodness, dear Lord, have Brother Andrew make the bread today and restrict Cormac to the vegetables." Left alone in the pantry I should eat more, I confess it; but no, I have enough. I'm just greedy.'

'Poor Brother Cormac. Is his bread so bad?'

'You haven't noticed? Father, you're a saint! He made the bread yesterday. Did it not sit in your gut like a stone?'

Father Peregrine forbore answering that question, and changed the subject.

'How are you finding the rule of silence, Brother? Some men find it disturbing and hard to live with at first.'

'Well...' Brother Francis glanced up at the abbot with a grin, then looked away into the fire. 'It wasn't so bad in the middle of winter, because my lips were too cold to move then anyway, but I... um... you must know I'm always in disgrace over my tongue—it has a life of its own it seems. Not only that, it chatters what's little worth hearing. "Half-witted and facetious babble" were the words Father Matthew used, and on that particular occasion I own he was not far wrong. I talk too much and jest too much—speak first and think later.'

'Well, that's honest,' said Father Peregrine. 'But silence—when you are silent—does not oppress you?'

Francis laughed. 'It is formidable at times, but then I am small-minded. I lie like a child in the night, counting sheep until I fall asleep at last, and then the bell is clanging and I am stumbling down the night stairs to Matins, drunk with sleep and cursing the day I ever heeded God's call. The silence then is a happy necessity, for if I were permitted to speak it would be only a drivel of self-pity and complaint!'

'Yes...' Father Peregrine nodded thoughtfully. 'It's not easy to get used to the night prayers and the broken hours of sleep.'

'Get used to it! By my faith, I had ceased daring to hope there would ever be a time when I'd get *used* to it! Will I?'

'Oh yes, you will adjust. Granted, it would be pleasanter to stay in bed, but it is not always as weary a business as at first.'

Brother Francis smiled. 'Then God be praised,' he said. 'I'll look forward to that.'

'Your fire is dying,' said Father Peregrine. 'Put some more wood on it.'

I must make this lad talk to me seriously, Peregrine thought as he watched Brother Francis placing the little logs on the fire. Things are not all roses. He has a low opinion of himself. He knows he's a trial to the man he works under... he thinks himself greedy... small-minded... a chatterer. There must be some conflict in a young man who bites his nails to the quick and can't get to sleep at night.

'I imagine,' he said, 'that the vow of celibacy you have taken is at times a stony path?'

Francis was silent for a moment, fiddling unnecessarily with the fire. He looked up at Peregrine with a wry smile, then he dropped his gaze again.

'I have learned,' he said eventually, 'to sit on my hands and say "*no*" and then ten Ave Marias and then "*no*" again.' He grinned sheepishly at the abbot, hugging his arms round his knees as he sat on the hearthstone. 'But stony, as you say.'

'That can be the least of it,' said Peregrine quietly. 'The hardest lesson is the learning to bring your capacities for tenderness— the heart of you—into a communion of trust with the other brothers. A celibate monk must learn how to be fruitful in his dealings with others—how to open himself to them in truth, and bear the pain of letting himself be seen, be known. Yes, your heart must truly have an unlocked door, or celibacy will sour you, wither you. It is not only a matter of the physical urge, though God knows that is not to be belittled.'

Francis raised his eyebrows. 'You're saying, in effect, "You think it's bad enough now, my lad, but you wait!"'

Father Peregrine smiled at him. 'Not exactly that, but no, it is never easy. There are ways, though, to lift this renunciation up out of the realms of mere denial into a beautiful giving of your self; a way of peace.'

The fire spat out a spark, and Francis moved back a little, and flicked it back into the flames. He sat tracing his finger through the ashes on the hearthstone as he took in this thought. Composed and quiet, half-smiling, his face gave nothing away.

I can't get near this young man. Father Peregrine thought as he watched him. He has made himself a fortress. Amusing, courteous, responsive, but too well-defended for his own good. Father Matthew's right, there is something about this eternal cheerfulness... a rebuff... no, maybe not. Maybe he is protecting something... a wound somewhere... .

'Brother Francis,' he said, 'are you aware that you have turned aside my every enquiry with a jest?'

Francis looked up in consternation. 'No, I—I'm sorry,' he stammered. 'I didn't mean to be rude, I—'

'You have not been rude. But I can be of no help to you if you keep me forever at arm's length with flippant remarks and an armour-plated smile. Now tell me honestly, since you are evidently not too troubled by any of the things I have asked you about, is there anything you *are* finding difficult?'

'Not... not really,' said Francis slowly after a moment's silence.

Father Peregrine shook his head. 'Let me put the question another way. I would be ten times a fool if I let you assure me that it is all plain sailing. What is it that you find hardest about your life here?'

Brother Francis stared at the ashes in the hearth, his face fixed into a slight, strained smile. He had hidden the secrets of his heart from others for so long it was not so easy to put his hand on them himself now when he wanted to. He did not speak for a long time.

'The constant criticism,' he said at last. He looked up at Father Peregrine, his face still protecting his heart with the habitual pleasantness of his smile. The abbot was observing him quietly and seemed not about to speak. Brother Francis swallowed. 'I know I have a long way to go. I know I talk too much. I know I am sinful and proud... and foolish. But, oh God I do try!'

His smile was gone suddenly, and the surface of his face was distressed with little twitches of nervous muscles that didn't know what to do now they were no longer employed in guarding his soul with the shield of a smile. 'I have studied and practised and done my utmost to please, but it is never enough. I am hemmed in by rebuke and censure until it seems there is nowhere left to stand. There is no place for me. I can *never* be good enough.' The words tumbled out and stopped abruptly. Quivering in the unaccustomed exposure, he looked at the abbot, his brown eyes full of distress.

Father Peregrine considered him carefully. 'Francis, you try too hard,' he said.

The young man responded with something halfway between a laugh and a gasp of indignation. 'Let me know when I've got it right and I'll stop,' he said bitterly.

'No, that's not it. It is the effort itself which is your undoing. It makes you unreachable. Father Matthew now, he feels as though you are, somehow… insincere… in some way false, maybe.'

Brother Francis said nothing, his face was quite still. I've hurt him, thought Peregrine. He was not ready for it. It went too deep. Help me now, good Lord, or this will close him up even more.

Francis looked away, gazing into the fire. 'Insincere?' he said quietly. 'Am I?' Slowly and absently he crushed one or two tiny sparks that lay on the stone, then he let his hand lie still. 'You have met my family, haven't you.' It was a statement, not a question. 'My father's wife is his second wife. She is not my mother. I was not quite seven years old when my mother died. My father married again not long after, and my stepmother brought me up after that. She did her duty by me, fed me and kept me clean, but… I suppose I was as irritating then as I am now. More so, if that be possible. She said no end of things to me along the lines of, "Why can't you…? Will you never learn to…?" and "For the hundredth time, child!" It must have been the hundredth time, too. It certainly felt like it.'

He paused and pushed the logs together on the fire, took another from the pile and placed it among them. His thoughts were far away. 'My mother, my real mother, I will never forget her. She was beautiful. I tried to paint her face when I was painting the picture of the Virgin that Brother Clement took such exception to—she with the offending smirk. She had gentle brown eyes, my mother, and she was always merry and kind. She

91

had the kind of laugh that made you laugh with her. She used to say to me, "Always do your best, my son. Be a good boy," and she'd rumple my hair and smile at me.'

He was silent, then, and Peregrine waited; waiting for the memories that hurt and haunted the silence to be spoken and released.

'She got ill a long time before she died. I don't know what was the matter with her. They didn't tell me then, and no one ever spoke of her after my father married again. It was as though she'd never been. They took me in to see her, the evening they knew she was dying. She'd grown so thin, her eyes big and her face white. She could scarcely speak. Just a whisper. She smiled at me though, even then. She looked as though the illness was hurting her badly, but she was smiling, for me; looking at me and her eyes were shining and kind still. She was not afraid. My father was standing behind me. I can remember it, because I wanted to go and kiss her—it was the last time—but he had his hands on my shoulders and restrained me. I suppose she was too ill. She stretched out her hand and touched my cheek, and she said, "Be a good lad for Mother now. Do your very best." They sent me out of the room then. It was late—dark—but I was sent to play in the garden. I stood out in the garden, looking up at her lighted window. I was cold. The next time I saw her she was laid out for burial.'

The sense of his suffering swelled out now that the protective layer he had covered it with was stripped back. The air was tense with his pain. His body was rocking slightly in the rhythm of rekindled grief. Softly, he said, 'And I *have* done my best. But somehow it is never good enough.' He grew still, very still, his face a mask of sadness.

'It may be,' he said at last, 'that my soul is... lightweight... not worth very much perhaps, but I give you my word, Father, I am not insincere. I have done my best.'

How odd it is, Peregrine thought, that men think the soul is invisible. Times like this, a man's soul sits about him like a mantle for all to see. I wish Father Matthew was here. He'd not now scorn this man as insubstantial froth.

'Your soul, my brother, is of inestimable worth,' he said. 'It is also of great beauty and nobility. It is only that you have kept it hidden from us. You have not understood. Your best is yourself. You are not a dog or a dancing bear that you must do tricks and search out ways to please us. The gift of yourself in trust—that is your best. You need courage to make that gift to us, because we also are weak in our humanity and will sometimes deal with you clumsily, as Father Matthew has, as Brother Clement has, as I have just now, without understanding, bruising you. Brother, please forgive us. Please trust us. There is nothing, nothing, nothing amiss with your conduct or your attitude. There is no rebuke here. But, be at peace. Breathe a little more easily. Allow us to see you, to know you. When you are bewildered and bowed down under discipline and hard words, weep—don't laugh. Father Matthew is not unkind, but he takes you as he sees you, and he believes he sees light-hearted indifference.'

'I can't weep!' Francis' voice was sharp with pain. 'How must I weep? I couldn't bear to weep. There is no one... it hurts too much... I could never stop... I can't weep.' His hand moved in a gesture of hopelessness, and he got up from the hearth and knelt before the abbot.

'Father, I confess my fault. I ask God's forgiveness and yours.' The words were torn wretchedly from the centre of him, little shreds of his soul ripped away in pleading need. He was trembling, his head bent, his hands clasped together.

Peregrine looked at him in perplexity. He's getting tighter and tighter in this pain, he thought. God help me, I'm not breaking it for him. What is it he fears? What is it he needs me to do?

'My son, what is it you want me to forgive? Are you asking me to *forgive* the pain of your heart? God knows—'

'*Me*,' Francis broke out in anguish. 'I need you to forgive *me*. I want to be clean. I want to be true... I want to belong to God... I want him to forgive *me*.'

Father Peregrine looked at the young man, the tightness of his hands, his shaking despair, the rigidity of his bowed shoulders and neck and bent head, and wondered what to do.

'I don't want him to leave me alone.' Peregrine heard the note of shame, of reluctance, and understood that this was the heart of the thing.

'I am so terrified he will abandon me. I don't deserve him, I'm not good enough, I'm not clean or pure or holy. I dread his coldness, his turning away... Oh, I'm so afraid of burning in hell. I would do anything, I... I am a desert place, useless and poor. Oh God, forgive me... forgive me... not only my sins, but *me*. Oh, do not leave me alone, don't abandon me... .'

'This is what you fear?' Father Peregrine asked him gently. 'Francis, look at me. This is the thing you fear? That God will abandon you?'

'Yes. How should he not? What is there of worth in me?'

Blindly, almost cringing in his need, he reached out his hands to Father Peregrine, and creeping forward he buried his face in the abbot's lap and allowed the brittle shell to shiver into a thousand pieces.

God of love, help me to drive out this fear, thought Peregrine as he stroked the young man's head and brooded over his grieving. However can I reassure him? He had seen many men weep in release; seen it bring them comfort and ease their sorrow, but this man's weeping was bitter agony. There was no peace in it, only pain. He thought of Father Matthew—'This eternal smile of his covers an emptiness within,' and resolved to listen to him more often.

'My child… my poor child,' he murmured. He did not know what else to say. He knew the futility of smothering this fear with platitudes about God's mercy and love. It is a thing a man needs to know deep in his heart, an understanding with God himself. That is what faith is. It cannot come second hand.

'It hurts too much. It's going to break me!' Francis gasped in terror. 'It's like a great black wave, towering too high. If I let it fall, oh God… I'll be dashed to pieces! It will destroy me!'

On the quivering shoulders Peregrine rested his hands, frustrated at their crippled immobility, wishing he could spread his fingers, hold the man through his fear.

'It will destroy you if you try to contain it,' he said. 'You must allow it to break. If it destroys you, well, I will be with you. There is no more holding it in, my child.'

There was a moment when the abbot felt the power of that black tide of grief rising in Francis' soul; when the two of them were arrested in the awe of the moment before it crashed. Then Francis' whole body convulsed like a man vomiting, his hands gripping desperately in the folds of Peregrine's tunic. His mouth was forced wide open in a silent cry of agony, his eyes screwed shut as the thing ripped through him. It left him sweating and shuddering, his mouth slack and trembling, his eyes dazed and dully oozing tears. He moaned softly like a labouring woman. Then, in the wake of the first crashing wave, poured out the flood-tide of his grief. The pathetic bravery with which he had fought it so long lay splintered like matchwood, floating dispersed on the dark sea that swept him away. There was no way now to combat the bitter sorrow or master the pain. It was too much for him.

'Oh…' Francis groaned in misery as he sat back on his heels, struggling unsuccessfully to compose his face and stop the tears. 'Forgive me the liberty. I… oh…' he hid his face in his hands, unable to contain his grief, bent double with the anguish of it.

Looking down at him, Peregrine realised then and forever that faith and peace come not from believing in God, but from the secret of God's love hidden in a man's heart. Surely, my God, he prayed sadly, you will fill this child's emptiness, have pity on his torment? Father Peregrine watched as Francis fought with his subsiding grief, finally managing to control it, straightened up with a sigh that was half a sob and spread his hands on his knees.

'There you are, then. This is me,' he said, with an attempt at a smile that wrung the abbot's heart. 'What now?'

Father Peregrine looked at him. He could think of nothing to say.

Francis turned his head aside and looked into the dying embers of the fire. 'The brotherhood of this community,' he said, his voice flat and tired in the sad, bruised finality of defeat, 'is like a lighted room in a house. There is the warm fire of life and fellowship on the hearth, and the brothers are gathered safely round it, and outside it is night. Out in the night is the lonely place of darkness and danger and fear. Do not bad men prowl in the darkness, and wild beasts? Out in the darkness, where no light is, you can stumble and fall on the stones, and the cruel thorns tear at you. I am here in the light and warmth of the house, but I belong in the darkness. I can't forget the darkness, it draws me. This light, this warmth, this brotherhood—it's not for me. I don't deserve it, it isn't mine. I'm here on false pretences. I don't belong.'

He looked desperately at Peregrine. He is tortured by this, the abbot thought. I've got to say something to help him.

'If you cannot put the darkness out of your mind, my son,' Peregrine said slowly, 'maybe you should face it. Open the door of the lighted room and go out of the house and look at the darkness. What is there?'

Francis hesitated. 'The restlessness of night. The silence, and strange sounds in the silence. Then—out there in the night, someone... a long way out into the garden, under those big whispering trees somewhere... there is someone weeping... sobbing... groaning. Father, there is someone in such trouble out there. I want to go and see!' His eyes widened. He was really seeing it.

'Go on then.' It seemed so real that Father Peregrine felt as curious as Francis did.

'Oh! There are stars. The darkness is not as black as I had thought. I had forgotten the stars. It's a garden with shrubs and trees, dark shapes. I can smell the perfume of the flowers. And someone is crying in the darkness in bitter distress. I can't find him. I'm searching for him, looking everywhere. Wait—there, under the trees. A man, crouching, bowed down to the ground. Oh, the loneliness of him. He's *broken*. He's—he's afraid. I've never seen a man in such despair... I must go and... oh, God, it's *Jesus!* Out here, all alone. Jesus... he was out here even before I came out. He was out here all the time, in the lonely place where abandonment and fear belong. He has always been here. I think it... it is Gethsemane.'

'What are you going to do?' asked Peregrine in fascination. Brother Francis looked at him incredulously. 'Do? Stay with him, of course. I can't leave him alone in this distress. I couldn't just abandon him. Jesus, my heart, my love... his courage is the hearth for the night. As long as he is here, the darkness is home. The outside has become the very centre. Jesus... my Lord, and my God.'

The tension and pain had drained out of him; his face was soft and rapt, lost in the vision. His eyes, no longer haunted, were brimming with wonder and tenderness.

There was something Peregrine wanted to know. He hesitated, reluctant to intrude on Francis' contemplation. Then he said, 'The door of that house—did you shut it behind you when you went out?'

'No. I was scared to go out. I wanted to leave a way back in. You can shut it behind me now. I'll be all right here.'

He knelt a moment longer, and sighed deeply, amazingly at peace. For a few seconds, time had tipped over into eternity, and they were in the place where angels come and go. Then Brother Francis looked up at his abbot with a grin.

'There's the Office bell now. My foot's gone completely dead, kneeling here. I'm going to have the most wonderful pins and needles when I stand up. I'll limp along to chapel with you if that's—oh I'm sorry, Father, that was tactless.'

Brother Francis blushed as the abbot bent to pick up his wooden crutch, stood up and leaned on it. Peregrine laughed at Brother Francis' mortified face as he scrambled to his feet.

'We'll limp together then, my son,' he said.

As they walked along the cloister, Father Peregrine glanced at Francis' face, which had the same intelligence and humour, the same firmness—everything the same but for red eyes and a red nose—but resettled now into a new context of peace. The same but all different. The same man but reborn.

'The Christ you saw,' said Peregrine quietly, 'that is the Christ I love. All his life he lived pressed on every side by human need, and he met the weariness and testing of it with a patience and humility that silences me, shames me for what I am. But in Gethsemane, I see Jesus crumple, sobbing in loneliness and fear, crushed to the ground, pleading for a way out. And there was none. I cling to that vision, as you will. That sweating, terrified, abandoned man; that is my King, my God. Such courage as I have comes from the weeping of that broken man.'

Brother Francis reached out one finger and gently touched the abbot's hand. They went into the chapel in silence, each to his own stall. Father Peregrine pulled his cowl up over his head, and sat gazing as he always did at the great cross that hung above the altar. 'How did you do it?' he prayed in silent wonder. 'How did you do so much without doing anything? How did you lift the man out of that torturing agony of grief and fear just by consenting to bear the same torture, the same lonely agony? Suffering God, your grace mystifies me. You become weak to redeem me in my weakness. Your face, agonised, smeared with dust and sweat and blood and spit, must become the icon of my secret life with you. The tears that scald my eyes run into your mouth. The sweat of my fear glistens on your body. The wounds with which life has maimed me show livid on your back, your hands, your feet. The peace you win me by such a dear and bloody means defeats my reason. Lift me up into the power of your cross, blessed Lord. May the tears that run into your mouth scald my eyes. May the sweat that glistens on your body dignify my fear. May the blood that drips from your hands nourish my life.'

Father Peregrine watched Brother Theodore take his place beside Francis, saw him rest his hand gently a moment on Francis' shoulder, having seen in his face the signs of recent tears. The abbot watched the shyness of the smile with which Francis acknowledged Theodore's gentleness. Ah! Yes! He has allowed himself to remain vulnerable, the abbot rejoiced. Then as the cantor lifted his head to begin the chant, Peregrine sped one last private prayer to the Almighty—'And of your goodness, dear Lord, help me to think of some sensible explanation to offer Father Matthew.'

'Deus in adjutorium meum intende,' and the brothers responded *'Domine ad adjuvandum me festina.'*

✠   ✠   ✠

Mother fell silent then. I looked at her, sitting in her chair in the candlelight, her hands folded quietly in her lap, her eyes still seeing people and places far away as she gazed at the candle flame.

'What do those Latin words mean?' I asked.

'Mmm? What?'

'Those Latin words you said at the end of the story. What do they mean?'

'They mean, "Oh God, come to my assistance. Oh Lord, make haste to help me." It's the versicle and response from the beginning of the Office.'

She sat a moment longer, thinking, then she said, 'I have always loved that story. It was that story which first taught me that we can offer no solutions, no easy answers, to other people's tragedies. We can only be there. It is Jesus they need, not us, and even he offers no answers. He offers himself. It is when people find their way through to him that the pain of their life becomes the pain not of death, but of birth. A thing of hope. Hark at me, rambling. It must be late—look, this candle was a new one and it's half burned away. Let's go downstairs. Therese and Daddy will be thinking we've fallen asleep up here.'

CHAPTER FIVE

Beholding the Heart

'Tell me a story, Mother,' I said one Sunday afternoon. We had been doing a jigsaw puzzle while the rest of the family were out walking the dog on the hill after lunch. 'Tell me a story about Father Peregrine.'

But the telephone rang just then, so I went into the kitchen to answer it. It was my friend Helen, wanting to know about our geography homework, what it was and whether it had to be in on Monday or Tuesday. While I was talking to her, there was a knock at the front door. I heard Mother opening it and saying, 'Hello, Elaine! This is a surprise. Come in.'

My heart sank, because I knew once Elaine got going she would probably talk for ages and ages. After I had finished my conversation and put the phone down, I went and popped my head round the door.

'Shall I make coffee, Mother?'

Mother nodded, but didn't speak, because Elaine was talking already. So I made three mugs of coffee and took them in. I thought that if I was there too she might go a bit sooner.

Elaine looked a bit pink-eyed and sniffy, as though she'd been crying. She was telling Mother that she had decided to leave our church.

'I didn't want to go without saying a word to anyone,' she said. 'Keith and I have prayed and prayed about this. Every time we open our Bible, it falls open at the book of Jeremiah, about how the people of God are deceived and idolatrous. I think God is trying to tell us something about our church.'

'Maybe...' said Mother cautiously. 'Of course, the book of Jeremiah is very near the middle of the Bible. It probably would keep coming open near there.'

Elaine shook her head sorrowfully. 'I wish I could think it was only that, but this morning in my Bible notes, the reading was from Jeremiah. It said, "Of all the wise men among the nations, in all their kingdoms, there is no one else like you. They are senseless and stupid, and they are taught by worthless idols." I don't think I can ignore it any longer. God's word to us is so powerful and clear. Keith and I have been longing—you know we have—for months and months for our church to move on with God, and it just isn't. The Holy Spirit isn't there. It's so dead. We have to face the fact that God has moved on and left us behind, and Keith and I want to move on with him. So we're going to start worshipping at Hill Street Baptist Church. We've been there a few Sundays, and the Holy Spirit is really moving there.'

Mother sipped her coffee. 'Do you really think God has left our church, Elaine?' she asked.

'I don't think he was ever there. Just look at it! Father Bennett's so awful and Father Carnforth's so old. We never sing anything but dirging hymns. We should be dancing and singing and raising our hands to God in praise. The Bible says we should.'

'Well, why don't you then?'

'Oh, don't be silly. You just *can't*. It's so inhibiting, so dead. You understand really, I know you do.'

'In a way, yes. I do like hymns though, and I can't see why Father Carnforth being old means that our church is dead, but I can see that Hill Street would suit you and Keith better.'

'It isn't a question of what we want for ourselves. If it was only us, of course we'd stay. It's what *God* wants that counts. It's been such a hard decision for us.' Elaine's nose went very red, and her eyes filled with tears. She blew her nose, and carried on, 'I haven't been able to sleep a single night this week, but God is moving on and he won't wait forever. Either you move with him, or you get left behind, and our church just isn't moving with him.'

Mother looked a bit sceptical, but she didn't say anything. She drank some more of her coffee.

'I've been thinking about what Jesus said to his disciples,' Elaine went on. 'He said that if anyone would not listen to their words, they must shake the dust off their feet and move on. Keith and I have been to Father Bennett and challenged him about the baptism of the Holy Spirit, and he was very rude to us.'

'You talked to Father Bennett about baptism in the Holy Spirit?' said Mother. 'My hat! What on earth did he say?'

'He just dismissed it. He said it was all a fad. He said all Christians had the Holy Spirit or they wouldn't be Christians.'

'Well, you have to admit, there is something in that,' said Mother.

'In a way, but *you* know there's more to it than that. It was you who first taught me about the Holy Spirit. So anyway, Keith and I have challenged him, and he has been confronted with God's word and rejected it. So we're shaking the dust from our feet and moving on with God.'

Elaine went quite soon after that. She didn't stay as long as usual. As she was leaving, the rest of the family came home, and then it was teatime and after tea Mother went to church.

At bedtime I went up and sat with her as she put the little ones to bed. I sat on the floor, watching the candle flame as it moved in the slight draught.

'Is it true what Elaine said, Mother?' I asked, once the little ones were settled down in bed.

'About what?'

'That God moves on, and won't wait for us. If we can't keep up with him, he'll leave us behind.'

'No. It's not true.'

103

'How do you know?' I needed to be sure. I felt a bit afraid at the idea that I had to keep up with God.

'I know because... well, if God moves on like that, who is it that picks me up when I stumble and fall? Someone does, and it feels a lot like Jesus. What about the story you wanted, Melissa? Shall I tell it to you now?'

'In a minute,' I said slowly. 'With the Bible... it is God's word, isn't it?'

'Yes,' Mother replied firmly.

'Well then, Elaine might be right, mightn't she? Jesus did say that thing about dust.'

'He said it, yes, but he said a lot of other things too that Elaine might more usefully take note of. A funny thing happens with the Bible, Melissa. It acts a bit like a mirror. People who come to it resentful and critical find it full of curses and condemnation. People who come to it gentle and humble find it full of love and mercy. The truth of God is not a truth like "cows have four legs" is true. God's truth is him, himself. There are no short cuts. You have to get to know *him*. If you try to use the Bible like a fortune-telling game, it just bounces your own ideas back at you. God won't let us use him like that. It's all right, Melissa. He understands our weaknesses and our mistakes. He does love us. He'll wait for us to catch up—even Father Bennett. He's not going to dump us like that.'

I sighed. 'Tell me the story. Whose story is it?'

'There's a bit of everyone in this one. Brother Theodore and Father Peregrine and Father Matthew mostly.'

'I like Brother Theo. Go on then.'

I lay down on the floor with my head on Beth's mattress, watching the candle flame as Mother began her story.

✠　　✠　　✠

People have different ways of protecting themselves. Brother Francis had chosen to protect his vulnerability with a smile. Brother

104

Cormac was like a hedgehog, making his soft belly invisible and exposing to the threatening world a back full of spikes. Both those ways are quite good ways of protecting yourself. They help you to cope when life's upsets seem more than you can face. But to protect yourself like that has a few drawbacks when the soft, vulnerable part of you has a wound. The hedgehog is wise to bristle against attack, but if his soft belly is wounded, sooner or later he needs to uncurl and let someone salve it, dress it, heal it. The one who, like Francis, hides his vulnerability with a shield, a mask, a smile, is protected more or less from wounding, but not of course from the wounds behind the shield—the wounds he already has. Sooner or later he has to lower the shield, to let the physician see and touch the sore place, if he wants it to be cleaned and bound up and soothed.

Father Peregrine's defence was his dignity of office—there was a certain refuge in being the competent, authoritative abbot of his community—but he too, for his soul's health, and for the sake of truth, needed from time to time to allow someone to see him, know him in his weakness and his human reality. There are, though, some people who—for whatever reason—cannot seem to protect themselves successfully, and Brother Theodore was one of those. He grew up through a miserable childhood in a home where he was a misfit, beaten and disliked; and he never found an adequate way of protecting himself. Francis had his smile, Cormac had his fierce bad temper, Peregrine had his aristocratic authority. Theodore had only his clumsiness. It was as though misery had numbed him. When a man's fingers are numb with cold or illness, he drops things, blunders, becomes butter-fingered—and that was Brother Theodore. Father Peregrine had found and touched and gently bandaged the wound behind the clumsiness; but of course we are what we are, and not even Father Peregrine could wave a magic wand for Brother Theo and change him instantly. For those like Brother Francis and Brother Cormac, once someone has been let near the hurting place, and allowed to touch it and help the pain, then their ways of protecting themselves against more hurt are quite useful.

But poor Theo and his disastrous clumsiness drew rebuke and trouble constantly, adding humiliation to pain, and insult to injury. Because, of course, his *soul* was not numb or impervious to hurt. He came perilously near to giving up on life, sinking into defeat, existing utterly without hope. Worst of all, in that most ugly face of despair, the despair of receiving love and affirmation, the little green plant of tenderness inside him all but withered and died, so that he could no longer *give* love. The wound almost cut too deep, and cut off life.

He was saved from this final despair by the joy of his work as a scribe and a musician, in which creativity his artist's soul flew free and rejoiced; and also by the understanding of his abbot, who kept him going. Father Peregrine patched up the cuts and bruises Theo's soul endlessly sustained, comforted his confused misery, delighted in his artistry, beheld his grief. It was a wonderful thing to Brother Theodore, that beholding. In his private meditations he would read the words of Psalm 139: '*Domine probasti me, et cognovisti me*—Oh Lord, you have searched me and known me,' and he would kneel down in the solitude of his cell whispering his prayer. 'Look at me, oh, look at me! Look at my sin, my failure, my stupidity. Oh, look at me and heal me.' And it was as he allowed his secret grief and shame to be looked at, touched and beheld by his abbot, that he was healed. It was not anything Father Peregrine did or said that healed Theodore so much as knowing that the abbot, whose body bore the scars of his own suffering, really did behold his grief. That somehow made it bearable.

For the period of his novitiate in the community, Brother Theodore and Father Matthew, the novice master, were each other's cross to bear. Father Matthew, that upright, stern, deeply religious pillar of monasticism was determined, though it cost him everything, to train Brother Theodore into an admirable figure of recollected piety. Brother Theodore, so far as Father Matthew was concerned, went from the novitiate into full profession as one of his failures. The mere sight of Brother Theodore was enough to pucker Father Matthew's austere brow into an unconscious frown of irritation. The encounter was indeed a costly one, but Father Peregrine knew what his novice master never understood: that it was Brother Theodore, not Father Matthew, who paid the price.

The abbot was, of course, a man of his time, and whereas a modern superior might have found someone kinder than Father Matthew to be the master of novices in his community, Father Peregrine accepted the severity of Father Matthew's régime as an important, if sometimes excessive, discipline. He contented himself with tempering its effects with his own mercy. He also suspected that much of Father Matthew's unyielding spirituality was made more of plaster than of rock, and to humiliate him by depriving him of his post might bring the noble edifice of his assurance to dust.

This particular day, when Brother Theodore was nearly, but not quite, through the tunnel of his novitiate year, had seen a good morning so far for both Brother Theo and Father Matthew.

The novice master had spent the greater part of the morning in the parlour with a family: mother, father and their son, who meant to try the life at St Alcuin's. They had come humbly for Father Matthew's guidance and counsel, which they received with a reverence and respect that was the more gratifying because they were of a lineage and descent that would have put them as far above Father Matthew's social aspirations as the sun in the sky, had he remained in the world as the fourth son of a struggling merchant. So St Alcuin's master of novices was feeling well-disposed towards all men as he emerged into the courtyard with his little party of visitors. Their talk had gone well. The lad was full of the wild hopes and ideals proper to a nineteen-year-old heart, and Father Matthew had smiled benignly on his avowal of vocation. He had smiled on the lad's parents too, for their coffers were lined with as much gold as silver, and more estates than any man could reasonably require. The abbey stood to receive a fair gift at their hands if their youngest son chose to make his soul as a monk in its cloisters. Even Father Matthew, whose vision was set unwaveringly upon heaven, could not help but notice these material benefits out of the corner of his eye, and feel a modest glow of satisfaction that their meeting had run so favourably.

He came into the courtyard with the three of them, and together they made a striking group indeed. Father Matthew's erect and ascetic dignity was enhanced rather than eclipsed by the fashionable elegance of his wealthy guests. Yes, things had gone well, and the small frisson of exultation he permitted himself was only diminished, not utterly extinguished, by the sight of Brother Theodore approaching, one sandal flapping awkwardly on a broken strap, the hem of his habit trailing and a smudge of livid green ink on his left cheek. Theodore was bearing in his hands a jug of beer from the kitchen, which was one of the ingredients of the ink he was mixing for his new project in the scriptorium ('*Beer*?' Cormac had said in the kitchen. 'Theodore, this had better be true.') which was just now absorbing him heart and soul.

He had one morning last week been summoned to the abbot's house, and found Father Peregrine seated at his table with a book lying before him in a little clearing amid the landscape of manuscripts and letters that cluttered his table. The abbot had greeted him with friendly courtesy, and then after a fractional hesitation, a split second of indecision, had taken the book between his hands. 'Brother, I would like you to look at this. It is a book of Hours that has not been completed. Do you think you can finish it for me?'

Brother Theodore heard the slight diffidence, almost shyness, and realised this was something special. He took the book and opened it. It was indeed something special. It was three-quarters completed, with fine and graceful lettering, and illuminations of subtle beauty, paintings of flowers and birds, of mythical beasts and intricate designs; a courtly dance of colour, balanced and harmonious, yet of uninhibited and arresting vitality. There were touches of gold shining on its pages, but used with restraint. This was not a vulgar riot of scarlet and gilt, but a sophisticated marriage of colours, and it was wanting a few pages still. As he turned over the parchments, which lay loose in a stack, unbound as yet because unfinished, he found there were two or three blank at the end, and one or two with the design sketched out, but not lettered or painted. There was one half-finished page with the lettering complete and the capital, but the margin half-done, started with the soft blue that was the theme colour for the page, but interrupted.

'Father, this is a beautiful thing', said Theodore, holding it in his hands, handling it with the curious mixture of confidence and reverence which denotes the true artist. 'It is... it is... I've rarely seen one so lovely as this. Indeed I would be honoured to complete it if you think I can, but where have you come by it?'

Father Peregrine had been watching Theodore closely as he examined the book, but now he looked down at the table, unnecessarily moving his pens, the ink, the seal.

'I had thought to continue it on the next Tuesday,' he said, looking up abruptly, his voice studiedly light. 'I had begun the painting of that last page on the Wednesday, then left it, with reluctance I confess, because the claims of Holy Thursday, Good Friday, Easter Eve and Easter Day left me with no leisure for anything. Then on the Monday night, they destroyed my hands. I put it away at the bottom of the chest over there, and it has stayed there this long time. Brother, will you be my hands? Will you finish it for me?'

Brother Theodore laid the little book on top of a pile of manuscripts on the table and turned over the leaves until he came to the half-painted one. He took it into his hands and studied it carefully.

'You think I can do justice to this?' he asked. 'If I had made a thing of such beauty as this, it would be no small sacrifice to turn it over to another man to finish.'

'These long months I have locked it away,' Peregrine said. 'It begins to look a little as though I thought it my own private property, which it is not. It is the community's, not mine to sit on like a dragon guarding its hoard. Of course you can do it justice. Your work is equal to mine. Besides, even if you could not, what of it? It is only a book.'

Brother Theodore had need to put a brave face on too much heartache in his own life to be fooled by this. He put the parchment back carefully among the others.

He cleared his throat. 'In the eighth Psalm,' he said, speaking in rather a hurry, his ears a bit red, embarrassed at seeming to preach to his superior, 'it says that God has put all he had made, all the works of his hands, into our care. I have often wondered what God felt—feels—when the beauty he has made and given us on trust is indifferently regarded; when men trap the singing lark and cut out her tongue for a dainty meal; when we beat little children with belts and sticks and let them creep hungry to bed to nurse their bruises; when we smoke out the bees and destroy them to rob them of their honey. God must have his head in his hands and weep sometimes, I think, in the heartbreak of our negligent misuse of his artistry, the work of his fingers. You understand what I'm saying to you? He knows, and I know, how you feel about this, even if no one else would. Can I take all of this away, not just the pages waiting to be done, so I can study how you've gone about it? Then I can do my best to make the whole thing a unity. Will you also write down for me the recipe for this blue ink, and I will try to mix some like it.'

Father Peregrine took a scrap of parchment from a little pile of torn remnants he used for jottings, and wrote down the proportions of the blue mixture. Theodore watched the toiling progress of the pen as the abbot formed the crabbed, unsteady letters. It was a laborious business: time and again the pen slipped in his crippled grasp, but the result was legible. He gave the slip to Theodore.

110

'Can you read my staggering script?'

'I can read it.' Theodore paused, then gathered his courage to say, 'To be your hands, that is a humbling thought, for your hands have more skill than you know. They have erased a lot of the black and ugly scenes from my heart and painted some fairer, brighter colours. Father, I will do what I can.'

So Brother Theodore had spent the week studying the little book, getting the feeling for its design, planning and preparing the last pages, practising lettering in the style Peregrine had used, and now he was ready to mix his inks and begin to paint the remainder of the half-finished page. It was to be a work of love, and the trust given him he hugged like a treasure to his heart— 'Brother, will you be my hands?'

As he walked along carrying the jug of beer to make his ink, his mind was filled with the vision of the page as it would be when it was done. The soft blue; blue of the Virgin's cloak, blue of the morning, blue of the woods in spring, of a child's eyes, of the harebells nodding in the summer fields... blue of all things gentle and beautiful and... Theodore looked up and saw for the first time the little knot of gentry standing in front of him. He was suddenly uneasily aware of Father Matthew's eyes upon him in the sort of mild disapproval that Brother Theodore knew from experience could be kindled into wrath as easily as dry grass in the drought of summer can be set ablaze. He felt the familiar flutter of panic at the base of his throat, the clutch of apprehension in the pit of his stomach, the tightening of his chest.

It was at that moment that Father Peregrine came limping out into the courtyard to find Father Matthew, and to extend his own greeting to the guests. He saw the family standing there making their farewells. He saw Theodore pause, then nervously approach with his head bent in an attempt to render himself invisible as he passed them on his way to the day stairs leading up to the scriptorium. He saw the expression on Father Matthew's face as Theodore stumbled over his broken sandal strap, shot out

111

his hand to save himself, and dropped the jug he was carrying. It was smashed into tinkling fragments on the stone, in a puddle of warm fizzing beer that splashed my lady's elegant gown and my lord's embroidered shoes. There was a moment in which the universe stopped to allow for Brother Theodore's mind to reel in dismay, Father Matthew's expression to change from mere resentment to red-hot rage, and my lady to step back with a little, affected 'Oh!' of alarm.

Theodore, speechless, went down on his knees in haste, gathering up the pottery fragments, dropping them again, cutting his finger on the broken shards. Father Matthew, his lips tight with fury, drew himself up to his full height and towered over the offensive wretch grovelling in the beer at his feet. Then Theodore's soul shrivelled under the excoriating shower of rebuke that the novice master released upon his head—his clumsiness, his discourtesy, the order and dignity of the abbey: it went on and on.

Smiling at the familiar scene (had he not often an occasion to bawl out his own serfs?) my lord took his lady's hand that she might step across the pool of beer, and the family moved discreetly away to allow Father Matthew to finish his scolding.

Theodore crouched on the floor, his hands filled with broken bits of pot and dripping with blood and beer.

Father Peregrine, when his novice master paused for breath, said quietly, 'Go gently, Matthew—he's shaking. There now, you neglect your guests. Leave him to me.'

After one last scalding reprimand, Father Matthew consented to rejoin, with a profusion of apologies, his guests thus abused by the clumsy foolery of his novice. They dismissed his apologies with gracious good humour as they moved away towards the gatehouse buildings across the abbey court. None of them looked back, except the boy. He glanced over his shoulder to see the abbot stooping down, trying with his twisted and awkward hands to pick up the last fragments of sticky pottery, and the young monk on his knees remonstrating with the abbot, dropping what he held already in his attempt to gather up what he had missed.

With an amused smile, the lad turned away and followed his parents into the gatehouse.

Father Peregrine pulled his handkerchief out of his pocket. 'Here, Brother, you have hurt yourself. Put that pile of pieces there to this side. Go and wash the cut on your hand and then you can find something to gather these up in. There now, don't distress yourself, it couldn't be helped. Swill away this spilled ale and there will be nothing left to remind Father Matthew of the offence.'

In mute distress, Brother Theodore did as he was bidden, and Peregrine went after Father Matthew and his guests to offer them the courtesy of an abbatial greeting.

When Theodore had disposed of the broken pot, and collected a broom and a pail of water, he returned to find Father Matthew standing there, balefully surveying the scene of Theo's disgrace.

'You will confess your fault of rude clumsiness at Chapter in the morning, Brother. I trust you are planning to wash this mess away. Have a care to leave no little shards of pot. What's this?'

He picked up a scrap of parchment which lay on the stone flags. Theodore thought at first he must have dropped his ink recipe, it was a little torn-off slip like it; but his recipe was safely tucked away in the scriptorium. It could not be. There was something written there, though. As Father Matthew read the writing on the little chit, his eyes widened and his eyebrows rose higher and higher. Brother Theodore watched him apprehensively. At last, the novice master looked up at him.

'Do—do you recognise this hand?' he spluttered. 'Whose drunken scrawl is this? Can a brother of this house be responsible for this... this... this... well, read it!'

So overcome was he with horror and disgust, that he held out the thing to Theo, who took it and read it with some curiosity. It was a poem, written in Latin. Father Matthew, having second

113

thoughts, twitched the parchment out of Theodore's hand. 'No, no, you should not be reading such filth. Heaven bless us, what a thing!'

But Theodore, who spent all his days working with Latin texts in the scriptorium, had scanned and understood what he read, which roughly translated as this:

This vigil is long.
What time I have sat here,
Watching the candle flame's
Slow, passionate exploration kiss the night.
The blind and gentle thrusting tongue of light
Finds out the secrets of the dumb receptive dark.
Her sensuous silence trembles with delight.

He did indeed recognise that drunken scrawling script. He had referred to it a dozen times that afternoon as he mixed up his pot of blue ink.

Father Matthew crumpled it in his hand. He was really shocked by what he had read.

'Did you recognise the hand, Brother?' he asked. 'To think that a monk should pen such words!'

'Maybe.' Brother Theodore hesitated. 'The young man who came to see you this morning stood here some while, Father. This is the kind of thing that young men sometimes write.'

Father Matthew was visibly relieved. 'Ah yes, it must be so! Then I shall give it to his father. The young lad's priest should know. His soul is in danger if he is prey to such sensual and lascivious ramblings.'

'No! Um... no, Father. Perhaps I should take it to Father Abbot. He should see it, surely? It may be that one of the brethren wrote it, after all, and besides, the lad plans to enter our cloisters. Father should know, don't you think?'

'Yes. Yes, Brother, indeed. I will take it to him after we have said Office. You are right.'

'I could take it,' said Theodore hastily. 'I am going there directly once I have mopped up this floor. I—I won't look at it again, I give you my word. I'll just take it to him.'

Father Matthew looked suspiciously at Theodore. Theo looked as innocent and submissive as it was in his power to do.

'I should like... I should like to confess to Father Abbot that I caught a glimpse of those words, and seek his counsel,' he murmured. It worked.

Father Matthew nodded soberly.

'Very well, but I charge you under obedience not to read it again.'

And he gave the incriminating verse into Theo's care.

Brother Theodore swilled away the spilled beer, his gut still swarming with butterflies as Father Matthew vanished from sight. Returning the pail with all speed lest the novice master should think better of his decision, he hurried to the abbot's house, and found Peregrine just setting off for chapel.

'Father, please, have you a moment? The bell's not rung yet.' Peregrine looked at him in surprise, and stepped back to admit him into his lodging. 'Yes, Brother?'

'Father Matthew found this in the cloister. I think you might have dropped it when you pulled your handkerchief out of your pocket this morning.'

He smoothed the crumpled parchment in his fingers as he spoke, and gave it to the abbot who took it and looked down at it. Peregrine took a deep breath.

'Father *Matthew* read this?' Never before and never afterwards could Brother Theodore recall seeing his abbot so completely disconcerted.

'What—what did he say?' Peregrine enquired, red faced.

'He was not too—he didn't appreciate its beauty, but he was generous enough to believe that no brother of ours could have written such a thing. He was happy to swallow the suggestion that the young lad who came this morning might like to write poetry.'

'You have read this?'

'But briefly. He asked me if I recognised the hand, showed it to me, then thought better of it, fearing to corrupt my innocence. He consented to let me bring it to you, and put me on obedience to look at it no more.'

'Yes. Well, he was right.' The abbot turned away and took the crumpled poem to his table, and put it inside his box of sealing waxes. 'I will burn it later.'

'No.' Brother Theodore shook his head. 'Don't burn it. He may have been correct, but he was not right. He doesn't know what life is; he doesn't know. He hasn't known what it is to be in black darkness, and won, revived by the tender wooing of light. He doesn't know. The filth is his; the poem is not filth. Don't burn it.'

'Filth? Is that what he said?' Father Peregrine pondered the judgement. 'I hadn't meant it so. It seemed a thing of wonder, that silent, lovely mating of the darkness with the light. A hallowed thing. I am sorry if I have degraded that loveliness.'

'Father...' Theodore begged, 'can I read it once more? Please. It was beautiful.' The abbot looked at him, torn between propriety and the understanding that lay between them. Then, 'Why not?' he said. 'You have read it once. The harm is done, if harm there be.'

Theo retrieved the shabby scrap and read it through.

'I'd like to put this at the end of your book of Hours. It is lovely.'

'You'll do no such thing! Put it away, Brother, the bell is ringing for Office. We must go. Thank you for saving my blushes.'

Theodore smiled. 'You've shielded me often enough. I need no thanks.'

When the midday Office and meal were over, Father Matthew went in search of his abbot. Peregrine braced himself for the interview as he heard the knock at the door.

116

'Father, might I have a word with you?' The abbot's stomach tightened into a knot at the discreet, confidential tone of his novice master's voice. He managed a pallid smile.

'Be seated. Have you come to talk to me about this verse you found?'

'You have seen it then? I trusted Brother Theodore to bring it straight to you. He is a sore trial, but he is honest, I believe. I was shocked and ashamed to discover evidence of such lewd and inflamed imaginings in this holy place. Brother Theodore wondered if it might be the work of the young man who was here this morning. If you think it may be so, I will take it upon myself to inform his confessor. The thought that it be not his, but may be the shameless fantasy of one of our brethren is almost too much to contemplate. Did you know the script?'

'Yes.' Peregrine looked at him helplessly. He moistened his lips with his tongue.

'Brother... the poem is mine.'

The weights and balances of all the world readjusted in the incredulity of Father Matthew's silence. A hundred angels shut their eyes tight and stopped their ears and held their breath in dread of his reply.

'*Yours?*' He was absolutely thunderstruck.

'Yes. I'm sorry it so distressed you. It... please believe I had not intended any lewdness. There is a place, in the mind of a man of God, for reverence of carnal love in its beauty, surely? As there is a place for Solomon's love canticle in the canon of Scripture.'

'The Song of Songs,' said Father Matthew coldly, 'is an allegory of the love between Christ and his church.'

'Well, I don't know...' Peregrine demurred. 'Solomon was a long time before Christ. It reads a bit more lively than that to me.'

Father Matthew shook his head sorrowfully. 'Sacred Scripture is then to be taken thus lightly? Compared with such verse as this thing you have written?'

'No. No, of course not. I didn't mean my scribblings were of that standard. Matthew, I'm sorry, I'm very sorry to have offended you. I don't know what else to say. I beg your pardon. It was not meant for anyone's eyes but mine. I'm sorry.'

'Sorry you wrote it, or sorry I saw it?'

It is possible to push a man too far. A flash of irritation shone a warning spark in the abbot's eye.

'Sorry you saw it, since you ask. I would never willingly offend you, you know that, but don't you think you are being a little bit prudish?'

A tremor shook Father Matthew's upright frame.

'I strive for purity in my innermost being,' he replied.

Peregrine sighed. 'Well, you've achieved it in good measure. Father Matthew there is nothing else I can say. I'm sorry, I beg your forgiveness. Is there anything further you wish to discuss?'

Poor Father Matthew. He retreated from his abbot's house a saddened and disillusioned man. He came that evening into Compline, and sat scowling in thought in his stall. What was the world coming to? His eye fell on the candle flame as it moved in the slight draught. He watched it, intrigued, as it dipped and swayed, swelled and pointed, shivered and moved in the air current. He watched the hungry urgency of the flame push against the gathering dark, and a tingle of unfamiliar life stirred somewhere inside him. 'Heaven help us, he's right,' he acknowledged reluctantly.

He paused by the abbot's stall as the brothers filed out of chapel, and almost spoke; but they were in silence, and it would not do to break the rule. Father Matthew lay awake in his bed for some time that night, troubled by a dim uneasiness. It was the closest he ever came to understanding that 'he came that we might have a proper code of behaviour' is not the same as 'he came that we might have life'. But he chose in the end to take refuge in sleep, murmuring the words from the 139th Psalm, *'Proba me*

Deus, et scito cor meum: interroga me, et cognosce spiritas meas.
Ei vide, si via iniquitatis in me est, et deduc me in via aeterna...
Examine me, O God, and know my heart: probe me and search
my thoughts. Look well if there be any way of wickedness in me,
and lead me in the everlasting way.'

The words that Theodore clung to for healing, Matthew
scoured his soul with before he tidied it away, clean, to sleep.
God, in his unfathomable silence was content for them each to
find what they could in his book. No doubt he also heard the
abbot's last silent meditations from the same Psalm.

For all these mysteries I thank you:
For the wonder of my being, the wonder of your works.
You know me through and through.
You saw my bones take shape
As my body was being formed in the secret
Dark of my mother's womb.

✠   ✠   ✠

It had never struck me before, the sensuous, very physical
intimacy of those words, but as Mother spoke them, I could
almost feel it, see it; the close, fluid world of the foetus, turning
in the darkness that changed from red gold to deep red, to velvet
blackness, depending on where the mother's body was. The silent
dance of creation, a symphony of mysteries woven together;
bone, sinew, skin. The hands of God hidden from sight, working
from the spirit outwards with absorbed tenderness, creating toes,
shoulders, shaping the cranium, the long curve of the spine, the
delicate intricacies of the lungs. Not to be despised, a human
being, in all its weakness and helpless desire, its clumsiness and
frailty. A thing of beauty, a work of God's hands. I glanced up
at Mother, but I felt shy to put into words the things that were

119

stirring in my soul. Instead, I said, 'I'll never look at a candle flame in the same way again!'

She smiled. 'No,' she said, 'but you'll look at it more attentively.'

CHAPTER SIX

God's Wounds

Mother and I walked slowly up the hill to church. It was a warm, still evening, the sun was sinking behind the trees. Their leaves had begun to turn yellow and a few were falling. Our church was built on the edge of the common land that led up to the cliffs, on the outskirts of the town; a little oasis of countryside undisturbed by the spread of housing estates.

The bell was tolling slowly for Evensong as we strolled along the church path, and the tower clock chimed the half-hour as we settled into our pew. Mrs Crabtree was there, and the Misses Forster, elderly twins who dressed the same in pale green macintoshes and grey suede shoes. Two rows in front of us sat Mr and Mrs Edenbridge, very upright and correct. She was very smart, as always, in a coat with a fur collar and a rather expensive hat. He was immaculately turned out in his grey suit, the bald dome of his head, above the snow white hair that fringed it, shining pink in the lamplight. Across the aisle, Stan Birkett the dustman was hurrying into his pew as Father Bennett swept out of the vestry, paused to bow ceremoniously to the altar, and then turned to face us, booming, 'Hymn number three hundred and eighty-one: "Crown him with many crowns." Hymn number three eight one.'

That was an ambitious hymn for Evensong, long and loud. I was glad Mrs Crabtree was sitting in front of us and not behind us as the congregation started to sing, and the enthusiastic dissonance of her voice made itself felt.

> *Crown him with many crowns,*
> *The Lamb upon his throne...*

A late wasp droned lazily across the church, its aimless, floating path carrying it to the pew in front of us. It settled there and walked about a bit. It stopped to wash its face.

> *Ye who tread where he has trod,*
> *Crown him the Son of Man,*
> *Who every grief hath known*
> *That wrings the human breast,*
> *And takes and bears them for his own...*

The wasp took off again, drifting towards the front of the church. Its flight carried it up towards Mr Edenbridge's right shoulder, and he suddenly became aware of its buzzing. He must have been one of those people who are afraid of wasps, because in instinctive recoil, he ducked his head and gave a little, hoarse, hastily-muffled cry, flapping his hymnbook at his shoulder. The wasp veered away, and dropped from view into the pew behind him. Mrs Edenbridge, who stood on her husband's left, was looking at him in surprise. He, oblivious to her astonishment, continued peacefully with the singing of the hymn:

> *His glories now we sing,*
> *Who died and rose on high;*
> *Who died, eternal life to bring*
> *And lives that death may die.*
> *Crown him the Lord of peace...*

The wasp arose from the pew again, ascending behind Mr Edenbridge's head. He could hear it, but not see it. He spun round in panic, beating the air about his head with his hymnbook. His wife stared at him in amazement. The wasp had changed course and was now sitting quietly on a pillar.

Mr Edenbridge resettled his glasses on his nose and glanced at his wife. 'Wasp,' he mouthed, silently. 'Wasp.'

She looked at him in blank incomprehension. Father Bennett, aware of an undercurrent of commotion among his flock, was eyeing Mr Edenbridge with disfavour over the top of his hymnbook.

'Wasp! Wasp! There's a wasp!' whispered Mr Edenbridge loudly to his wife, who was rather deaf. She looked around, looked down behind her, looked behind him. He too began to look around for the wasp. It was nowhere in sight.

Then it came sailing across in front of Mrs Edenbridge, and she jumped backwards in alarm. Mr Edenbridge lashed out at it hysterically with his hymnbook, but it dodged him and flew away.

Crown him the Lord of love;
Behold his hands and side—
Rich wounds yet visible above,
In beauty glorified...

'Hrrmph!' Mr Edenbridge cleared his throat, and applied himself to the hymn again. He had seen Father Bennett watching him, suspiciously.

All hail Redeemer, hail!
For thou hast died for me;
Thy praise shall never, never fail
Throughout eternity!

The wasp was sitting innocently on the rim of the lamp overhead, washing itself.

'Dearly beloved...' began Father Bennett in forbidding tones. I picked up the prayer book and looked hard at the words of the prayer, quelling with an effort the giggles rising inside me.

'Whatever was the matter with Mr Edenbridge tonight?' asked Mother as we walked down the church path afterwards. I looked back up the path. Father Bennett, standing on the doorstep to bid his congregation 'Goodnight' as they departed, was offering Mr Edenbridge a distinctly cool handshake.

'Oh, Mother, didn't you see it? There was a wasp!'

'Is *that* what it was? No, I was concentrating on the hymn. It's one of my favourites: "Rich wounds yet visible above, in beauty glorified." I love that one. So it was a wasp. Poor man. Father Bennett was looking rather sourly at him by the end of the hymn.'

'Father Bennett couldn't see it. Mother, will you tell me a story? There's time, walking home.'

'All right then. I'll tell you a story if you make me a cup of tea when we get in.'

'Mother! I always do!'

'I always tell the stories. Have I told you Brother James' story? No? I didn't think so. He wasn't Brother James yet, at the time of this story. It was before he took his first vows. His name was Allen Howick. It was singing that hymn tonight that reminded me of this story. It's about the wounds of Christ.'

✠　✠　✠

Allen Howick was born in the year 1295, and throughout his childhood was loved—adored even—as the only child of his father and mother. He grew up into a fine, handsome, young man, whose mother denied him nothing, and whose father, a silversmith, a master craftsman, intended to bequeath to his son all his treasure, all his skill and all his business acumen. Allen enjoyed a privileged status in the small society in which he lived (the parish of St Alcuin's on the edge of the Yorkshire moors, served from the Benedictine abbey of that name). He was a wealthy, well-fed, well-favoured young man. By his twentieth year, he was a much coveted prize as a husband, and there were no fewer than five lasses making sheep's eyes at him at Mass on Sundays and dreaming about him in bed at night. In short, he was a big fish in a small pool, thoroughly spoiled and wanting for nothing. He had everything. Life had nothing left to give him that he hadn't already got, and he was peevish, discontented and bored. The village lasses, eager to win him as a husband, had tried to put a little on deposit by securing him as a lover. He'd had them all and they were nice, but he had to confess, with a certain sense of amazement, that even sex bored him now.

He came up early to Mass, one Sunday morning. He was out of sorts and more than a little hungover from a party the previous night. It had been his birthday and he had celebrated in style. Now he had twenty years behind him and a foul taste in his mouth.

One of the brothers (it was Brother Francis) was opening the great doors of the abbey church as Allen walked up the stone steps. Allen had never really noticed Brother Francis before, but he supposed he must always have been there. Francis, on the other hand, well knew Allen and his family, knew it had been his birthday and was surprised to see him out of bed at all. One glance told him what Allen had been doing the night before and that its legacy this morning was a thick tongue and a muzzy head. He grinned at him. 'Fine morning,' he said pleasantly. 'Been celebrating?'

There was something in the innocent enquiry that caused Allen to look at him suspiciously. He flushed slightly, put on his dignity by the twinkle in Brother Francis' eye.

'Yes, if it's any of your business,' he retorted, and stalked past him into the church.

He sat hunched up in his family bench, and watched Francis as he walked purposefully up the aisle, his cheerfulness evidently undented by Allen's rudeness. Francis disappeared through a door in the north wall of the church, and Allen was left on his own.

The spring sunshine streamed gloriously through the great window at the eastern end of the church, and he could hear birds singing. From further away the bleating of sheep carried on the wind. Otherwise, all was quiet. Allen looked around the huge, empty building. Usually among the last to arrive and the first to leave, he had never been there on his own before. Lord, but it's peaceful here, he thought, as he gazed about him. Wonder how much it cost to build it?

As he rested in the great hollow shell of tranquility and light, listening to its silence, it dawned upon him that 'empty' was the wrong word for this place. It was as full as could be: full of silence, full of light, full of peace. There was something about it that was almost like a person. It had—almost—its own speech. He lost the sense of it as people began to arrive in dribs and drabs, and the speaking silence was erased by their murmured conversation, the creak of the benches, the occasional stifled laugh, the shuffle and tap of shoes on the flagged floor.

The Mass was attended by the well-to-do and the respectable; farmers and merchants for the most part. They came in their Sunday finery, their wives on their arms, their sons and daughters around them. Their servants were expected to attend first Mass at five o'clock, and were busy making Sunday dinners and doing the household chores by this hour of the day.

Allen's parents came into the church and sat down beside him. It was not like him to be early to Mass, but they knew better than to ask questions. Rosalind Appleford, the wool merchant's daughter, shot a coquettish glance in Allen's direction as she passed. 'God give you good morning, Allen Howick,' she whispered, pouting her lips just a little for his benefit. Allen raised a wan smile, then looked the other way. His obvious rejection stung her, and Rosalind began to regret last Wednesday evening, which she had spent in his arms.

'*Dominus vobiscum*,' the cantor raised his voice in the chant.

'*Et cum spirito tuo*,' responded the brothers in the choir, and the people of the parish in the nave.

Allen yawned. He found the Mass tedious. It was a question, in the main, of trying to avoid reproachful feminine eyes and enduring pangs of hunger. He sat or stood or knelt with everyone else through the rite of penance, the liturgy of the word, the abbot's homily; but his mind was sunk in indifference, in the contempt of familiarity.

'*Pax Domine sit semper vobiscum*'

'*Et cum spirito tuo*,' responded Allen automatically. Then, like a far away song, like a weak shaft of sunlight on a December day, something roused in his soul. '*Pax Domine sit semper vobiscum*. The peace of the Lord be always with you.' Peace. Peace. He thought of the huge serene peace of the building as he had sat waiting for the people to arrive. Was it then possible to have that vast peace *inside you?* He had always assumed the words of the Mass to be a polite ritual, designed to humour a remote deity, keep him happy, keep him remote. But this—'the peace of the Lord be always with you'—this invited the far-off God right *in*. Peace. Allen was not sure what peace was. He was not sure if he'd ever known it. He wondered vaguely if his father would permit him to convert the guest bedroom into a chapel, maybe pay the abbey to send one of the monks there to say Mass for him, so he could have that peace on hand, at home when he wanted it. It would be good to spend a spare moment sitting in the quiet, enjoying the peace of God.

One of the lads from the abbey school was singing the *Agnus Dei*, his voice trembling slightly in the dread of public performance.

'*Agnus Dei, qui tollis peccata mundi, dona nobis pacem.* Lamb of God, who takes away the sins of the world, give us your peace.'

Allen felt as though something was wringing the inside of him. Suddenly, angrily, hungrily, he knew he didn't have peace. He had everything else, but he didn't have peace. He thought of Brother Francis; that cheerful, purposeful manner, unmoved by his own surliness. Peace, yes, it sat about that monk like it clung to the stones of these walls. How had he come by that peace? What had it cost him to get it?

Allen went up with the straggle of communicants and took the bread on his tongue, the body of Christ. 'Give me your peace,' he prayed. Sitting on the bench through the final prayers the words repeated in his mind: 'Oh Lamb of God, who takes away the sins of the world, give us your peace.'

He spoke to no one as he left the church and walked home. All his life, whatever he wanted, he had asked the price and it had been his. What was God asking for his peace? Lamb of God, you take away the sins of the world... that, it seemed, was his price. He wanted Allen's sin, in return for his peace. It seemed like an easy bargain. Allen thought over the past week. Wednesday night with Rosalind. Well, that was sin. Pleasant, but sin. He thought of his party the night before... luxury, drunkenness... the wasted food thrown to the dogs. In fact, the more he thought about it, the harder it was to think of anything in his life that did not bear the taint of sin. Did God want the whole of it, then, before he would part with his peace?

Allen was irritable all that day. He slept little that night, and on Monday morning sat pale, moody and silent at his workbench in his father's shop.

'What's biting you?' asked his father, as he set out his tools at his own bench. 'You look like a jilted lover.' He glanced questioningly at Allen. Maybe one of the lasses had made her mark. It was about time. He picked up the trinket he was working on, and bent his head over it.

'It's not that,' he said. As he looked at his father, Allen felt a fluttering of apprehension. What he was about to say was unlikely to be well received. 'It's not that,' he repeated, a little louder. There was an edge to his voice that his father had not heard before, and Master Howick looked with attention at his son. Allen cleared his throat nervously.

'I'm going to be a monk at St Alcuin's,' he said.

His father stared at him in disbelief. 'You've lost your wits,' he said at last.

Allen shook his head. 'No.' His father was still staring at him, waiting for him to explain.

'I want God's peace,' Allen said, feeling foolish.

'God's peace? Can't you have it here at home? It's free, isn't it?'

'Is it? Have you got it?'

His father blinked. 'Me? Yes, of course. Well, I don't know. Peace? I never thought about it.'

There followed two weeks of arguments and scenes, but in the end Allen's determination overrode his mother's tears and his father's hurt bewilderment. His heart was set on the monastic life, and he meant to have it, as he'd had everything else he took a fancy for.

Allen went to see the abbot. He did not enjoy the interview. Trained to the craft of the silversmith, Allen's hands were dexterous and precise tools, and he found the sight of the abbot's maimed, almost useless hands disturbing, revolting. The long scar that extended all down the side of his face looked horrible too, and his jerky gait as he limped along with the aid of a battered wooden crutch, the foot of it padded with leather to silence its tapping progress, reminded Allen of the bogey-man of his mother's nursery tales. His wounds and the fierce hawklike look of his face, with its dark eyes that seemed to pierce a man to the soul, frankly terrified Allen, but he made his request and was told that he, like any young man, was welcome to try the life.

So Allen Howick kissed his girlfriends goodbye, and dutifully embraced his parents. He would prefer to walk up to the abbey

129

alone, he said. There was nothing to be gained from their company. He turned, embarrassed, from his mother's tears, and filled with an almost intolerable mixture of elation and dread, he walked away.

His mother and father watched him go, their only child.

'It's worse than if he'd died,' his mother whispered. 'How did we fail him? We gave him everything.'

'Not peace,' replied her husband, with heavy sarcasm.

Their son turned the corner of the road without looking back.

✠   ✠   ✠

Allen found life at St Alcuin's gruelling. The night prayers, the meagre food, the hard work and the silence all combined to make him irritable and weary beyond endurance. The other young men in the novitiate, Brother Damian and Brother Josephus, had both taken their first vows and seemed to know their way about and behaved with an easy nonchalance that grated on Allen's strained nerves. He could not wear the habit of the order until he too took his novitiate vows, but he was given a plain, coarse, black tunic similar to the brothers' clothes to wear, and his own soft wool and fine linen were given into Brother Ambrose's care, in case he should change his mind and leave. Neither a brother nor the worldly lad he had been, Allen was alone in a no man's land between two worlds. Father Matthew, the novice master, he hated. Allen had never bothered much with his studies, knowing that his passage in life was assured, and he felt degraded by Father Matthew's detection and scrupulous exposure of his academic and spiritual weaknesses. The bitterest pill of all was the very public business of confessing his faults, kneeling on the ground, begging the brothers' forgiveness for such trifling matters as offending against holy poverty by losing his handkerchief.

He lay at night, sleepless on the rock-hard straw bed. 'Peace!' the night mocked him, astir with Brother Thaddeus' earth-shattering snore and Brother Basil's troublesome cough, and the gibberish mumblings of Brother Theodore's dreams; 'Peace!'

In spite of it all he sensed something. He didn't know quite what it was, because he didn't have it himself, but he sensed something in some of these men: an assurance, humour, tranquillity—hang it, peace! How did they get it? Allen ached for it.

He could feel it in the abbot, though he was afraid of him. He could not analyse it. In the brief moments of the one or two occasions he had dared to return the gaze of those dark grey eyes, Allen had glimpsed unfathomable depths of sadness, resignation, warmth... a mixture of things, and behind them all an extraordinary vital gladness that didn't fit with the lameness and disfigurement. Somewhere, Allen reflected, as he worked in silence at his task of book-binding, that man is saying 'yes' where I am saying 'no'. But yes to what?

'How did Father Columba get his scars?' he asked Brother Josephus one evening as they sat in the novitiate community room for the hour's recreation after supper. He had been only eleven years old when the abbot was crippled and his hands were broken, and he had not been interested in the village gossip of adult life in those days.

'Who? Oh, Father Peregrine. He was beaten up by enemies of his father's house eight—no nine—years ago.'

Allen digested this information. He wanted to ask another question, but hated to look uninformed. His curiosity got the better of him eventually: 'Why do you all call him Father Peregrine?'

Brother Josephus grinned. 'Well—does he look like a hawk or a dove?'

'What?'

'Columba—his name in religion—it's the Latin word for a dove. After Saint Columba, of course, but that's what it means. His baptismal name was Peregrine.'

131

Allen thought about it. 'He... he scares me,' he admitted, surprising himself with his own truthfulness.

Brother Josephus looked at him in astonishment. 'Father Peregrine scares you? Why?'

Allen began to regret his honesty. 'I—I feel as though he can look right into my heart,' he mumbled.

Brother Josephus laughed. 'It's not him you're scared of then. You're scared that what's hidden in your heart will be found out. What are you hiding?'

Allen stared at him for a moment then looked away. 'I think I'll go down early to chapel and be in good time for Compline,' he said stiffly, and made his escape.

In the choir, one or two of the brothers knelt in prayer in the twilight gloom. Father Peregrine was sitting in his stall, the scarred face shadowed by his cowl, his maimed hands resting still in his lap. Allen couldn't tell if his eyes were open or closed. He hurried to his own place and knelt there. The silence of the choir seemed oppressive, a great, swollen stillness, weighing down on him. He was glad when, ten minutes later, the bell began to ring for Compline and the community filed in and filled the shadows with the music of their chant.

Then, silence again, the deep, deep silence of the night, the Great Silence that took a man down with it and would not let him ignore the doubts and fears that daylight business crowded out.

Allen slept fitfully, as always, and felt bone-tired in the morning. After first Mass he trailed up the stairs to the novitiate schoolroom. Father Matthew greeted him with the information that Father Abbot wished to see him that morning to discuss his progress. Allen turned round and plodded back through the scriptorium where the scribes were already busy with their copying and illumination work, and down the day stairs to the cloister. He met Brother Theodore on the stairs. One of the fully-professed brothers beyond the small world of the novitiate,

Allen didn't know Theodore very well, but the quick appraisal of Theodore's glance discovered his weariness, and there was something comforting in the smile he gave Allen as he passed.

Allen was relieved to have escaped a morning studying the latest arguments for and against predestination, but he was not looking forward to being alone with the abbot. He hesitated outside the door of the abbot's lodging, which was as usual ajar, then knocked. He walked into the large, sparsely furnished room and shut the door behind him. The abbot was at his table, reading through some documents.

'A moment, and I shall be with you, my son,' he said, and glanced up at Allen momentarily. Then he looked up again, his attention arrested. 'Faith, boy, you look weary. Don't sit on that stool. Fetch the chair from the corner there. You need something to lean on, by the look of you. I won't keep you but a minute.'

Allen fetched the chair and sat on it, watching Father Peregrine's face as he finished the perusal of his documents and then put them aside. The abbot smiled at him, and the kindness of his smile, in that fierce, uncompromising face, took Allen by surprise.

'Well? Hard going?'

The frank sympathy with which he spoke brought sudden, completely unexpected tears to Allen's eyes. Hard going? By all holy, it was hard going! He blinked the tears away furiously, but didn't trust himself to speak. He stared hard at the inkstand on the table, determined not to betray his exhaustion and turmoil.

'My son, why did you come?' asked Father Peregrine, quietly. That, at least, Allen could answer, and the moment perilously close to tears was over.

'I came to find God's peace,' he replied.

The abbot nodded. 'Have you found it?'

Allen looked at him, wearily. This man could see right into him. He could see that, couldn't he?

'You know I haven't found it.'

'Do you want to go on looking, or have you had enough?'

Allen thought. To go home... home to a good fire, a soft bed, a bath whenever he wanted one. Home to his mother seeing to all his needs, to lying abed in the mornings sometimes... to an undisturbed night's sleep.

'But if I go now...' Allen paused. 'Well, where would I go? I can't spend the rest of my life walking away from it, can I? I couldn't bear it. I don't... I don't really feel as though I have a choice. Apart from that, yes, I've had enough. More than enough.' He felt the lump rise in his throat again and thought he'd better stop talking.

'If it's any consolation,' said Father Peregrine, 'which it may not be, I felt very much as you do. And... God turns no one away. He will give you the peace you crave.'

Allen leaned forward in his chair. 'When did you—how did you find it?'

The abbot smiled, 'It'll give you little comfort if I tell you. I found the peace of God, really, surely, for always found it, just nine years ago. I was forty-seven. And I wouldn't recommend anyone to find it the way I did.'

Allen looked at him in horror. 'Forty-seven!'

Father Peregrine laughed at him. 'I'll pray for you, my son, every day, until you find the peace of God. I know what it is to hunger for it, believe me.'

He talked to Allen a little longer, asked some more questions, let him talk a while, then said, 'Father Matthew will be chiding me if I keep you longer from your instruction. He says... he feels you can do with as much schooling as you can get.'

'Thank you, Father.' Allen got to his feet, and returned the chair to its corner. He felt obscurely encouraged. This rather alarming man seemed to know, and care, how he felt.

'Forty-seven,' he said as he put the chair down. 'God's wounds, that's a long time to wait.'

He turned towards the door.

'Just a minute.'

Allen looked back at the abbot, and was startled. Father Peregrine's eyes were ablaze with anger, his mouth set like a trap. He looked furious. Allen's jaw dropped. He stared in astonishment.

'If I *ever* hear you speak of the wounds of Christ again with such blasphemous levity, I will have you flogged, I give you my word.'

'Oh. Sorry,' said Allen, stupidly.

'That is not how we say it here,' replied his abbot, still angry but not quite so furious.

Allen knelt hastily on the stone floor. 'I humbly confess,' he said, as he had learned to do, 'my—my blasphemy. I ask your forgiveness Father, and God's.'

'No doubt God forgives you, and so do I. Now get up off your knees and hear this.' The abbot was still very angry. Allen stood up bewildered. Whatever had got into the man? It was only a figure of speech.

'Christ Jesus your God,' said Peregrine, fixing him with the fierce eyes that had made most of the brethren quail at one time or another, 'was mocked by the Roman soldiers. They blindfolded him and beat him with sticks, laughing at him, saying, "Who hit you then, prophet?" They stripped him naked and then dressed him up as a king. They crowned him with a cap of thorns. They flogged him until he bled, and they had him carry his cross on that bleeding back through the streets of Jerusalem until he fell under it. He lay on the torn skin of his back on the cross, and stretched out his arms and suffered the soldiers to hammer nails through his wrists. Nails that hurt him so… that convulsed his hands into claws. Have you ever wounded your hands, boy?'

Allen shook his head. He had never wounded anything, beyond the grazed knees of childhood.

'It is *hideous* pain. It is *agony*. Do you remember what he said—Jesus—the words he prayed as they hammered nails into

135

his hands on the cross? Well? What did he say—or have you forgotten?'

Allen moistened his lips nervously. 'He said, "Father forgive them."'

'Yes. Would you have said such a thing in that moment? No. Well may you shake your head in silence. Nor would I. Five years, ten years later maybe, but not then. The pain of it... I would... I would have begged, not for their forgiveness, but in terror, for mercy. I... did. They hoisted him up on the cross. A crucified man, my son, dies of suffocation from the weight of his own body. Three hours he hung there, shifting his weight from the nails through his feet to the nails through his wrists, scraping his flayed back on the wood of the cross. He did it because he loved us. He chose it, wanted it. It was the price of our peace. I say again: if I *ever* hear you make light of his wounds with your blasphemy, I will have you beaten until your back bleeds as his bled, and leave you to imagine the rest.'

'Father, I'm sorry. I didn't mean to offend you. I didn't think. I...'

'Whatever have you been thinking about while you've been here then?' Peregrine roared at him. Allen stood, silent.

'Well? What have you been thinking about?'

Allen felt as small and scared as a five-year-old. His well-fed, well-dressed, handsome, popular self seemed as far away and unreal now as something from a dream. Trembling in his coarse black robe in the blaze of this frightening man's indignation, he felt utterly wretched.

'I suppose,' he said, in a very small voice, 'I've been thinking about myself.'

'Tell me then,' said Peregrine, the quietness of his voice no more reassuring than the roar of the moment before, 'about yourself.'

Allen felt a trickle of sweat run down his back. Whatever was he supposed to say? The dark, fierce eyes were holding him, compelling him.

136

'I thought if I gave God my sin, he would give me his peace. It says it in the Mass, that the Lamb of God who takes away the sins of the world gives us peace. But—all my life seemed to be sin. I gave it to him by coming here.'

'So. That is what you thought and what you did; but you, tell me about you. You, whom Christ died for. You've been thinking about yourself, you say. Tell me then.'

Allen looked at him helplessly. 'I don't know what to say.' The abbot's silence gripped him like a huge pair of hands, and shook him.

'I...' he began huskily, 'I used to think of myself as something special. My mother and father dote on me. I had everything: clothes, money, horses, everything I wanted. Women, too. There were several... five—there were five girls. I used them shamelessly for my pleasure. I used my parents too. There was not... never has been... any gratitude in me. Nor reverence. Nor respect. But I didn't see it. You want to know what I am? I couldn't have told you until now. I'm a spoiled brat.'

He stopped, caught unawares again by the lump in his throat and the tears in his eyes.

'Thank you for answering my question,' said the abbot. 'As far as I can see you have answered it truthfully. You can go, then.'

Allen looked at him in horror. The tears threatened to overflow. Don't leave me like this, he wanted to plead. You've stripped me of everything. I can't face the brothers in the shame of this nakedness.

Father Peregrine met his look, looked right into him. Allen had never met a man who could look at him like that, unwavering, unembarrassed, without any inhibition at all.

'If you're going to weep, weep,' said the abbot. 'All of us do, sooner or later. You can forget any foolish notions you may have about your personal dignity when you stand as you are before Christ. Weep, then. Let him heal you of your ingratitude, and

137

your heartless abuse of love, and your using us to achieve your own selfish spiritual ends.'

Allen wept. The bluntness of the rebuke pushed him off the edge of the composure to which he had been so precariously clinging, and he fell down and down into the loneliness of his shame. First reluctantly, then miserably, then in an abandonment of shame and disgust, he faced himself and his own sin. Not even a villain, much less a hero, just a conceited, self-centred, ungrateful lad; unexceptional, lazy and spoiled. All his vanity and artificial dignity crumbled into ruins about him, leaving him wide open, unsupported, undressed. The world he had always known seemed to draw away from him, until he stood in a great empty tract of desolation. The nothingness, the falsity of all he was, bled out of him until it filled the vast, bleak desert of his loneliness, and he was engulfed in emptiness, hopelessness; lost. There was nothing left but the abandonment of his sobbing, which embarrassed him in its uncontrolled noisiness, until not even that mattered any more.

He had never felt so alone in his life, as he stood in the middle of the stone floor in the great, comfortless room hearing the noise of his weeping, hot tears coursing down his face, consumed in loathing of himself and all he had been. All the while he was aware of the presence of the abbot, neither condemning nor consoling him, watching and understanding the depths of his shame, such utter abasement, such a seeing of his own sin and strutting foolishness. Even to be stripped naked and stood in the market-place to endure the sniggers of passers-by would not have exposed him as the roots of his soul were now exposed. It felt as if it would never stop. He would have thought it was unbearable, except that he was too filled with shame to think anything about it at all.

'Help me.' The words came out brokenly, indistinctly, through his tears. He was unsure if he was addressing the abbot or God. Neither of them answered him, and in the end came the weary misery of the moment when his weeping had finished and there was nothing to do but find his handkerchief and blow his nose, dry his eyes and raise his head at last to meet the eyes of the man who sat in silence watching him. He was no longer sure what he was, who he was. Gutted of all that he had affected, all that he had taken for granted, he had nothing left but his wretchedness, his tired, hungry body, the coarse simplicity of the tunic that clothed him and the distressed unevenness of his breath. So he allowed his eyes to meet the abbot's grey eyes, and saw there profound sadness, and deep kindness, and a compassion that clothed him again, gave the nakedness of his soul some protection against the harshness of pain and humiliation. Allen drew in his breath and let it go in an exhausted sigh. He drank in the comfort of the abbot's compassion, of his evident understanding, but he could think of no words to say now. He could not begin to know how to move forward from the holocaust he had fallen into and start to live again; speak, act, move.

'Sit down,' said Father Peregrine. He picked up the wooden crutch and got to his feet. 'Sit down and gather yourself together again. Wait for me here. I'll not be long.'

Allen watched him as he limped across the bare austere room, his jerky gait, the awkwardness of his twisted hands as he leaned on the crutch and with both hands grappled with the great iron handle of the door. It occurred to Allen that this man had good reason to understand humiliation, and was well acquainted with suffering. Formidable he might be, but the most imposing man in the world would be overwhelmed at times by that level of disability. While he was wondering whether to help him. Peregrine conquered the door handle, and glanced across the room at Allen before he went out. Allen's soul, stripped and washed clean, was still plain in his eyes, as clear and clean as a new sheet of parchment ready for use. The first thing written there was concern for Peregrine as he struggled with the door. Nothing patronising; insight. There was a flash of understanding between them as their eyes met again. Each had glimpsed the other's humiliation, met it with compassion, felt it as his own.

'Wait for me,' said Peregrine again, and left Allen sitting alone, trying to make sense of all that he had just been through. It was as though he had just crossed the rapids of a turbulent, flooding, wild river, and was cut off for ever from the further bank on which he had lived his whole life until now. He felt as tender and naked as a newborn; as exposed as a creature that had lived all its days underground and then found itself astonishingly, painfully, in the air and dizzy light of the mountains. No doubt about it, it was a costly, hurting thing. His soul, used to covert ways and sly disguises, was sore in the breeze and brightness of its new climate, but... there was something about the very pain of it that was more exhilarating than anything he had found in the comfort and ease that had padded his life so far. Allen gave up trying to understand it, and waited, wrapped in a sort of light-headed tranquillity of exhaustion.

It was not long before the door opened again, and Father Peregrine entered, with Brother Cormac in his wake carrying a large slab of pigeon pie and a mug of ale. Cormac glanced round the room and, locating Allen in his chair in the corner, brought the food over to him. He looked down at Allen's blotched and swollen face with a cheerful grin. 'Hungry?' he said. Hungry? Allen was becoming so accustomed to feeling hungry that he had almost ceased to notice it, but as he caught the smell of the food, he felt ravenously hungry, and his mouth watered for it.

He devoured the pie and downed the ale, which was not diluted this once, with single-minded absorption, while Brother Cormac chatted comfortably to Father Peregrine about the progress of planting in the vegetable gardens behind the kitchen.

'Thank you,' said Allen gratefully, as he gave the plate and mug back to Cormac, having chased up every crumb of pastry and drained every drop of ale. Brother Cormac took them with a smile, and there was something in his look which made Allen feel that here was someone else who understood very well indeed what he had been through, and knew just what it felt like. Allen returned his smile, wondering fleetingly if it was in this that brotherhood and peace had their roots, the losing of everything.

Father Peregrine had returned to his chair behind the table with its untidy heaps of books and parchments. 'Thank you, Brother,' he said to Cormac as he disappeared with the crockery, then he turned his attention back to Allen. Allen felt as warmed and fed by the kindness of that look as he was by the pie and ale that comfortably filled his belly.

'Now go to bed,' said the abbot, 'and go to sleep. Sleep all you need. Get up when you're rested.'

Allen looked at him in amazement. His whole body longed for sleep, *ached* for sleep, but he couldn't quite believe his ears.

'But—Father Matthew...' he said doubtfully at last.

'Father Matthew is not the ogre he seems. Nor, incidentally, am I. Leave me to speak to Father Matthew. You go to bed.'

Allen went to his cell and collapsed in sweet relief onto his hard bed. He felt drained and utterly spent, and he fell asleep instantly.

He was woken by the Office bell. He went down the night stairs to the choir, to discover to his amazement that it was time, not for the midday Office, but for Vespers. It was nearly supper-time. He had slept all day.

Brother Francis was the reader for the day. It seemed a long, long time since that Sunday morning when Allen had met him at the church door before Mass. He was reading from the book of Isaiah.

'*Ipse autem vulneratus est propter iniquitates nostras, attritus est propter scelera nostra; disciplina pacis nostra super eum, et livore ejus sanati sumus.* He was pierced through for our transgressions, crushed for our iniquities. Upon him was the punishment that brought us peace, and by his wounds we are healed.'

Allen felt as though the words were turning him inside out. Now he was rested and fed, he was able to look beyond the confusion of misery and shame that weariness and hunger had compounded into abject desolation.

'Upon him was the punishment that brings us peace, and by his wounds we are healed.' Timidly, hungrily, humbly, Allen's spirit reached up, yearned towards God. Wave upon wave upon wave of peace swept through him, cleansed him, comforted him, healed him. As he walked out of Vespers to the refectory for supper, he was bathed in peace, alight with peace, overflowing with peace.

Father Peregrine smiled as he watched him go.

After supper, Allen went up to the community room where he found Brother Josephus and Brother Damian. Brother Damian broke off his impersonation of Father Matthew discoursing on the beatitudes to look at Allen in amazement.

'God's wounds!' he said. 'Whatever happened to you?'

'Oh, don't say that,' said Allen. 'I'm sorry, I don't mean to sound like an abbot's chapter, but don't swear by God's wounds, Brother Damian. He... they... the wounds of Christ are the most precious thing the world ever saw. Don't make a blasphemy out of them.' He blushed, embarrassed and shy; it was so thoroughly unlike himself that the two young brothers stared at him.

'I'm sorry,' said Brother Damian, 'I didn't know it mattered that much to you.'

✠   ✠   ✠

We had reached our house before Mother came to the end of her story, and sat down on the steps to finish it uninterrupted. We stayed a moment longer, without speaking, watching the splendour of the sun going down, and then both looked round as we heard the sound of the front door opening. It was Daddy, holding his car keys.

'Oh, there you are, you two. I thought you'd got lost; I was coming to look for you. What on earth are you doing there?'

Mother got up and smiled at him.

'Enjoying the peace,' she said. 'But I'm ready for a cup of tea.'

CHAPTER SEVEN

Holy Poverty

Mother stood in the kitchen, reading through the letter Beth had brought in from school. She looked anxious and harassed as she glanced up and caught my eye. She waved the piece of paper at me.

'They never let up, do they? Beth's class is going on an outing to the estuary to see the geese and the other waterfowl, and just look how much money they want for the cost of the trip! Pocket-money recommended, for heaven's sake! Dear, oh dear, I don't know. She'd not get more than that for her birthday! What else? Some sensible outdoor shoes and a waterproof coat; a packed lunch and a warm sweater. Well, I can manage the lunch and the sweater, but she hasn't got a waterproof coat, and she's only got sandals. She hasn't grown out of those yet. I was hoping to wait until the weather gets a bit colder before I buy her winter shoes. If I get them now she'll outgrow them before the spring. Do your Wellingtons still fit you, Beth?'

Beth shook her head glumly.

'No? Your feet must have grown, then. It doesn't show so much with sandals. Oh, goodness me, Melissa, she'll have to borrow your kagoul and roll the sleeves up. That's waterproof. All that money, though! Why, it's as much as it costs me to feed her for a week. How many children are there in your class? Thirty-two? They're going to spend all that money taking you to see some ducks on a puddle of water; and we live by the sea!

What's wrong with seagulls, for heaven's sake? A whole month's housekeeping that would be for me.'

She sighed wearily. 'You'll have to wear your sandals and they can just lump it. You can take some spare socks in case you get yours wet. I suppose your class has an outing too, Mary, and Cecily's playschool. All right, never mind. You'll probably come home with a photocopied outline of a duck to colour and a vivid memory of someone being sick on the bus, but I daresay your teacher has spotted some educational value in it that I can't see. Out you go into the garden to play for a little while. I'm not quite ready with tea yet.'

There was never any money to spare in our house. We had two meals a day, apart from our breakfast porridge, and bread featured very prominently in one, and potatoes in the other. Mary and Beth came home from school for dinner in the middle of the day, because Mother said she could feed them at home cheaper than either school meals or sandwiches. Daddy said Mother was the only cook he knew who had hit upon the novel idea of using meat as a garnish. Our clothes were almost always second-hand, and so were our books. The little ones had some money for sweets on Saturday, I did a paper-round for pocket-money and Therese worked on Friday evenings at a local supermarket, filling shelves. We didn't mind not having much money, but I hated Mother having to be anxious about school trips and new shoes, and getting through the last week of the month before Daddy was paid.

'It's all right,' she would say, 'but choosing between baked beans and toilet rolls defeats me. They go together, don't they?'

Worst of all were the weeks before Christmas, when she would be nearly in despair trying to get together enough Christmas presents for all our relatives and friends.

'What a *silly* way to celebrate Jesus, homeless in a manger,' she said crossly. 'Although, I don't know. We'll be more or less down to milk and hay ourselves by the time we've paid for all this lot.'

Yet somehow, we always managed. 'There is nothing in

my life,' Mother said, 'that has taught me so much about the kindness of God and the reality of his love watching over us as not having enough money. He has never let us down. Never. Well, sometimes we have to ring up and say we'll pay next week, but nothing worse than that. I don't know what we'd do without him.'

'Without God?' Mary asked, puzzled. 'We couldn't do anything without God because we wouldn't be here at all.'

My mother was a resourceful woman, not easily defeated, but worrying about money was one of the few things that would reduce her to tears. More often though, when she was anxious, she would be bad tempered, irritable and sharp with us all. It was at the end of a week like that, that Beth's letter about the school outing came.

I got out the loaf of bread and the pot of blackberry jam for tea while Mother read through Beth's letter again.

'It's not bad really,' she said, 'and it's a month off yet. Perhaps she'll be able to have some shoes.'

'I wish we were a bit richer,' I said, getting the margarine and cheese out of the fridge, and bringing knives and plates to the table.

'I don't,' said Mother. 'I know it sounds odd, but I don't. I couldn't bear the thought of people who have no homes and are cold and hungry, if I always had enough. I know I get cross and upset about it, but I would be no better off for covering up my weakness with money. It's good for me to know the places where my soul falls down, and it's good to have to lean on God and ask for his help. I know it's not very nice for you when I'm ratty, but maybe it will help you to understand people better than you would have if you'd been too protected from the realities of life. There's another thing of peanut butter if you look at the back of the cupboard.' Mother poured tea into mugs for everyone except Mary and Cecily, who had glasses of milk. 'I know a story about poverty. I'll tell you it after tea, if you like. Call the girls in now. Where's Therese? In the living room? Oh, I didn't hear her come in.'

After tea, the three little girls had their bath, and then I read Cecily the story of the Great Big Enormous Turnip. Beth and Mary had heard that story too many times, so they went upstairs for a chapter of a book with Mother. Cecily made me laugh, her blue eyes getting rounder and rounder as I said, '... and they pulled and they pulled and they pulled and they *pulled* and they PULLED!' Without her realising it, her mouth was silently mimicking mine as I spoke the words of the story.

'... and the little mouse came and pulled the cat, and the cat pulled the dog, and the dog pulled the little girl, and the little girl pulled the little boy, and the little boy pulled the old woman, and the old woman pulled the old man, and the old man pulled the *turnip* and they...' I looked down at her, and she said the words with me: 'pulled and they pulled and they pulled and they *pulled* and they PULLED, and...' Cecily looked at me, her eyes dancing with delight. '*Up came the turnip!*' she shouted with me. 'And they all had turnip for tea, all of them. I hate turnip!'

I hugged her, but she wriggled free and raced upstairs to Mother. In the bedroom, Mother took her on her knee. 'Prayers, Cecily,' she said. Cecily put her hands together and shut her eyes so tightly that her face was trembling with the effort of keeping them shut.

'Gentle...' Mother prompted.

'Jesusmeekandmildlookuponalittlechild,' gabbled Cecily. 'Pity... pity... pity mice...'

'Pity my simplicity. Suffer me to come to thee,' Mother finished off for her. 'There, into bed.'

She drew the curtains and lit the candle as Cecily nestled into her bed. 'Go away, Cecily,' muttered Beth irritably as Cecily snuggled up against her.

'Lie still now,' said Mother. 'Ssh. I'll sing you a song.'

She sang them some songs, an Irish folk song and two hymns,

and they were quiet and drowsy when she had finished.

'Story?' I said.

'Oh yes. About poverty. This is not a story about the sort of poverty where people are in rags or starving. It's about holy poverty, monastic poverty.' Mother laughed. 'I once knew a girl who went to stay with some Poor Clares in their monastery. She came back all big eyes saying, "They live in such poverty! They only have *one towel* in the bathroom."

'"It must get very wet," I said. "Oh, no," she said, "they've got lots of bathrooms." Yes, holy poverty is different from the ordinary sort. It's simplicity, really. Having a humble and frugal way of life for the sake of Jesus because he was poor and like a servant. To live in holy poverty is one of the three monastic vows. The hardship of holy poverty is almost the opposite of ordinary poverty. With the ordinary sort, the worst thing is having no choice, being trapped in it. With holy poverty, the hard thing is being faithful to it, having chosen it.

'Anyway, this is the story. It's one that Father Peregrine's daughter Melissa used to love especially.'

✠   ✠   ✠

'I 'ave brought a little cask of wine with me, mon père. Exquisite, beautiful wine. If one of your young men will bring it to your house, we will sample it together. I made the mistake of drinking your wine last time I was here, bon Dieu! Hedgerow vinegars made of every curious root and flower the wilderness spawns. Sacré bleu! Your father would turn in his grave to see what you have descended to! And the foul mixture you drink with your viands—your ale and water—ah, Lord have mercy! There is time enough for purgatory. I have no wish to begin it now.'

Père Guillaume from Burgundy had come to pay Father Peregrine a friendly visit while he was in England. The two of them were walking across the great court of the abbey from the guest house to the refectory, which was the point of entry into the cloister buildings. Brother Martin, the porter, watched them from the gatehouse with a smile as they went slowly across the court, for they made an extraordinary couple; Guillaume strolling in corpulent magnificence (twenty-one and a half stones, Brother Martin decided, would be a very conservative estimate), and Peregrine's spare, nowadays slightly stooping, frame jerking along with the aid of his wooden crutch. To Brother Richard, the fraterer, who had caught sight of their approach through the window of the refectory and opened the door for them, they presented an equally amazing sight. Père Guillaume's voice was suave and educated. His eyes took in everything around him with quick intelligence, missing nothing. Great waves of rich laughter rumbled up from his enormous gut, shaking his immaculately shaven chins as he took Peregrine to task for the severity of St Alcuin's simplicity. His elegant white hands gestured articulately as he spoke.

At first glance, Father Peregrine's ungainly figure seemed unlikely company for such a man. That Peregrine's ascetic preferences and the frugality of his house horrified the abbé was the first thing obvious from the words that rolled across the court before him in the deep and fruity accents of his confident voice; the voice of a man used to commanding, used to imposing, used to power. But as they drew closer, Brother Richard saw that there was more to it than that. Père Guillaume bent his head and listened with close attention to Father Peregrine's quiet replies, and looked sideways at him with a sort of fascinated respect. And well he might, thought Brother Richard, as he held the door open for the two abbots to pass into the refectory, looking at the lean, uncompromising lines of his superior's face, disfigured by its cruel scar, illumined by the disquieting penetration of the dark, direct grey eyes. Well he might.

Father Peregrine stood aside to allow his guest to precede him through the doorway. 'Mais non, aprés toi, mon ami I must follow my betters!' The abbe stepped back, raising his hands in deprecation, then courteously but firmly put his hand to Peregrine's elbow, steering him ahead of him through the door.

Abbot Peregrine smiled his thanks at Brother Richard standing holding the door for them and Père Guillaume stopped to acknowledge him too: 'Ah, now; see how your sons love you, mon père! In my house they slam the door in my face. "Let the old pig root for his own truffles," they say. Yes, mon fils, 'tis true, I swear it!' He nodded at Brother Richard's startled face, then put a plump hand on his shoulder, the gold of his ring glinting in the sun that slanted through the doorway. 'I am jesting, maybe, but I speak the truth when I say that I am not loved as this abbot of yours is loved. The reign of God is in your love here. I love him too.' He patted Brother Richard's shoulder, and continued on his way into the room, where Peregrine stood waiting for him, watching Brother Richard's reaction with amusement. But the abbé stopped short. 'Mon Dieu!' he said, the sweeping gesture of his hand inviting them to look at their refectory. 'Look at the bare wood of this place! Have you no linen for your tables? Have you nothing better than stone for your candlesticks? Ah, but they are beautiful candles. I remember Frère Mark and his bees. Beautiful candles! They tell me, mon père—can it be true?—they tell me that these Englishmen are barbaric. Come, you are a Frenchman, you can tell me if it is true! They tell me it is impossible—but impossible—to stop the English from wiping their knives and blowing their noses on the tablecloths. It is true then, mon père. It must be true, for you have taken their tablecloths away!'

He stood in the middle of the room, his eyes wide in mock horror and amazement, his hands spread and his eyebrows lifted in enquiry. Peregrine laughed at him. 'For sure it is true, but I didn't take them away. Our novices stole them to enable them to escape over the wall at night, driven to despair by the insupportable harshness of our regime. Come now and revile me in my own house. Stop offending the silence of our cloister.

Alas, I have only bare wooden chairs to offer you there too, but I see you've thoughtfully provided your own cushioning as well as your own wine. Brother Richard, if you have a moment to spare, would you be so kind as to bring us from the guest house Père Guillaume's cask of wine? I have nothing he can bear to drink. Even the water in our well is rank, though it be sweet enough for our degraded palates.'

'Ouf! Touché!' the abbé chuckled. 'Very well, then, let us tiptoe along your cloister. Let me amaze you with the revelation, we too keep silence every now and then. I can bear to cease my chatter till we are within your parlour.'

So saying, he folded his hands reverently within the sleeves of his habit, and proceeded with regal dignity along the cloister, his face composed into a grand abbatial solemnity which went oddly with the gleam of mischief in his eye.

Brother Richard brought the wine, and broached the cask. He poured it out into the simple pottery beakers that were all the abbey could boast for drinking vessels. Father Peregrine saw the expression on Père Guillaume's face as he looked at the beakers, and forestalled his comment. 'Guillaume, it *suits* us to make pots. It keeps our idle hands from mischief. We make them, and then because we are barbaric as you say, and have but the clumsy manners of peasants, we drop them and break them. Then we can make some more and it saves us from mischief again. If we drank from silver vessels, we should have nothing to do but drink all day, and nothing to drink anyway, but ale and water. Thank you, Brother Richard. Your very good health, my brother, my friend. May God unite us in peace.'

'Amen, mon ami. Bon santé!'

'Oh, but Guillaume, this is beautiful wine. You have brought me the best. I am not so boorish yet that I cannot appreciate this. It is *beautiful* wine!'

Abbé Guillaume smiled in satisfaction, and looked affectionately at his friend. 'I have looked forward with impatience to this visit with you, mon frère. I carry you in my heart, though I see you seldom. It is an honour to be your guest.'

There was a knock at the door, and Brother Tom entered quietly. Brother Richard had sent him: 'He has a guest, Tom. Someone important, I think. He may need you to wait upon them.'

Père Guillaume looked round to see who had entered the room, and when his eyes lit on Brother Tom, he put down the beaker of wine which looked so incongruous in his elegant hand, and heaved himself to his feet.

'Frère Thomas! Mon ami! You remember me? You, I shall never forget, never! I see you as if it happens *now* before my eyes, standing like a prophet of God over that Augustinian snake, storming at him as the gravy dripped from his furious face. Ah, Sancta Maria, that was a moment to remember! Let me embrace you, mon fils!'

He enfolded Tom in a mighty hug, soundly kissed him on both cheeks and stood back with his hands on Tom's shoulders, beaming at him fondly.

'"I had rather be"—what was it? A beetle? Mais non, a cockroach! "A cockroach that crawls on the floor in the house where my abbot is master than be the greatest of those who serve under you!" Formidable, eh? I salute you, Frère Thomas. It does my heart good to see you again. May he have some wine, mon père? Is it permitted? Un tout petit peu?' He turned in enquiry to Father Peregrine, who hesitated.

'Truly, Guillaume, this is not how we usually spend the afternoon; but yes, why not. Sit down and share some wine with us, Brother.'

'Let me pour you some, mon fils, into this enchanting little pot. It is not at its best; it should settle, it should breathe, but never mind. Voilà. I have given some to your abbot, to draw the English damp out of his soul. The fog has penetrated him. He has become a little chill, a little grey. This will put the laughter back in his eyes—eh bien, look at him! You see! That frozen pond of

151

austerity is melting at the edges. You will drink some more of my wine, mon père? But a little. Non? Un soupçon?'

'Guillaume, this will not do. You can afford to roll unsteady into the Office, but I lurch like a ship with the side stove in as it is. Leave me with a rag of dignity to cover my foolish soul. I'll not go down to choir drunk, breathing fumes of wine with every phrase I sing. Oh, don't look at me like that. I meant no rebuke. We'll drink some more wine over supper.'

Abbé Guillaume nodded mournfully. 'It is as I thought. You have seen through me. "'Ere is a man," you say to yourself, "with all the virtue of a cracked pot." Fear not, mon frère, the comparison suggests itself to me quite unbidden. There is nothing amiss with this one. "He has suffocated his spirit, which was, alas, noble, in folds of flesh, and I must be wary of the contamination of his gluttony. What is more, I must shield this young monk from the debauchery of his ways, and in no way seem to condone them." N'est-ce pas? Eh bien, tu as raison, mon ami. Your abstinence is my reproach.'

He smote his breast and hung his head sadly, then burst into roars of delighted laughter at Peregrine's discomfited silence.

'Ça va, mon ami, je comprends. I will leave you to your dreary labours until supper-time, but you must promise me then to put aside your dignity of office and be my companion, my old friend, not my judge. I have a conscience of my own to make me uneasy— yes, still, I swear it—I will not be needing to borrow yours. You have finished, Frère Thomas? How do you find my wine? Ah, it has lit in your eyes a little candle. Pleasant? Yes, I think so too. Perhaps your good abbot will send you to France to visit me one day. I have a whole cellar full. What did you say, mon père? What was that very ungracious muttering? You think not, is that it? Ah, well, Frère Thomas, you would have been welcome. Tant pis, uh?

'With your permission, mon père, I will feast on the delights of your library until Vespers. I will behave impeccably, as solemn and recollected as your extraordinary novice master. À bientôt.

You will be with us later, Frère Thomas? Yes? Bon! You make an excellent cockroach! À bientôt.'

As the abbé left the room, taking his colour and laughter with him, and Brother Tom followed him out, Peregrine was left alone. The abbé reminded him of all the world he had left behind, the wealth and sophistication of his youth. To leave it all had seemed a clear call, to which he had responded with an unhesitating 'yes', but... it was true, maybe he was a little chill, a little grey... a bit negative, perhaps.

For the first time in years, his single-hearted conviction wavered. Oh God, if it were all a hollow edifice, this life he had built. If the gamble of faith were a losing bet, and the temple he had made of his life prove only an echoing vault, an empty house of death; all the sacrifice of chastity, poverty, obedience be no more than frustration, denial, loneliness. He shook the doubts away. There was work to be done. He must go to the infirmary to spend an hour with the aged bedridden brothers. There he forgot himself for a while in their company and conversation, but his mood of uncertainty and uneasiness descended again as he made his way slowly to chapel before Vespers.

He sat in his stall in the choir, the abbot's stall, centrally placed in the position of dominance for the man who carried the weight of status and power. When first he had come here, there had been a certain thrill in occupying that place. Pride... ambition, I suppose, he thought sadly as he sat there now. What a struggle it has been. What a struggle to fight the pride of my spirit on the one hand and the rebellion of my flesh on the other, and still to lead with confidence—to teach and shape the men given into my trust. He sat motionless, unblinking, looking back over the way he had travelled. What am I become now? he asked himself. The sour defender of my own crabbed asceticism? Is all that I have endured in the name of humility only the symptom of my own vain pride?

He thought of the merciless indifference with which he had driven himself in the early days: the hair shirts, the scourgings and fastings, the perverse satisfaction in his body's miserable craving for softness, for comfort, for pleasure, for tenderness. What was it for? And then, the bleak and barren desert in which he had fought to come to terms with his disablement, the grim tenacity with which he had striven to prove again his competence, his ability to rule, to lead.

He thought back on a day, one among many, when with a certain cruel detachment, he had very deliberately knelt to pray, brutally forcing the shattered knee to bend, letting the sickening waves of pain force his self-pity and distress into the background, so that the dizzy sweat of it hurting won a savage victory over threatening tears. Why? Systematically he had stripped the life of his community of all pretensions, all luxuries, all self-indulgence, seeking the poverty that God had promised to reward with the kingdom of heaven. He saw again the suffering of men he had held to his own standard: Brother Tom, half-frozen, prostrated on the threshold of the abbey in the biting winter dawn; Allen Howick, now Brother James, drowning in his shame, his poverty of being. 'I thought it was for you, my Lord,' he prayed uncertainly in an anguish of self-doubt. 'Was it not so? Was it the conceit of my spirit? If so, the most cowardly sensuality would have been a better choice. Let me not be a sham, my God. I had thought I had shaped a place of peace. I want your poverty.

'Oh, a pox on it all, I am tired of trying. Cling to me now, my God, for I have lost the will to cling to you.'

He tried to concentrate on the psalms, the prayers of Vespers; tried to ignore the insistent questions—'Why? Why? Why can I not be as Guillaume is, to laugh and drink and eat and forget? Why can I not forget the poverty of Gethsemane, of the cross? Nails! Nails! Oh my Jesus, my Lord... your love has won me... and how should I forget?'

At supper with Père Guillaume that evening, he toyed absently with his food, and he had little heart for conversation. Brother Tom, seeing his superior out of sorts, made himself as unobtrusive as possible as he waited on them. Père Guillaume observed his old friend shrewdly. He loved him. He had never understood his brooding intensity, but marvelled at his hunger for truth, for simplicity, for holiness. He tried to lift his friend's mood, to entice him out of his despondency, but without success. In the end he decided to take the bull by the horns.

'Is it your heart, your liver or your soul that is afflicted, mon frère? Your good brother has made us an excellent repast—these delicious little cheeses, this crisp salad—it is not all suffering under your roof. But you do not taste them. You are looking at your supper as if it has done you wrong, and you are pausing only to decide whether to flog it or excommunicate it. Will you not tell me what troubles your heart? You have the face of a thundercloud. You will give yourself indigestion.'

Peregrine did not reply. He tried to pick up his beaker of wine, but failed, as he often did, to straighten his fingers sufficiently to get them round the vessel. He gave up the attempt, and lifted it to his mouth with both hands. Brother Tom realised that both he and the abbé had stopped breathing as they watched him struggle and fail. Tom hurt for his abbot as he took the thing into his hands. I never knew a man to hate his own weakness so much, he thought.

Peregrine looked at Père Guillaume over the rim of his beaker as he drank. The stormy intensity of his eyes made the abbé stir uneasily. They had been the best of friends from youth, but despite all the years he had known him, the depth of passion he saw in Peregrine's eyes still made Guillaume feel uncomfortable, almost afraid. Peregrine set down his wine and pushed his plate of food away.

'Guillaume, am I a posturing fraud?' he asked abruptly. 'No, don't smile at me. You have mocked me this day long for my efforts at holy poverty. What humility I have, I tell you straight, is too frail to bear the weight of many gibes.'

Abbé Guillaume looked at him with dawning comprehension. 'Ah, so *that* is what it is! Mon frère, I apologise. Would that I

155

had the quickness of compassion you have, to see another man's distress. I had never intended that my idiot buffoonery cause you pain.'

'It's not your idiot buffoonery that hurts. That just makes me laugh, and heaven knows I can be melancholy enough. You do me good. No, it's not that. It's the thought that all I had hoped was humility, might be no more than my own stiff-necked pride. That's what hurts. Am I a Pharisee, a—a shell of religion, a loveless hollow of vanity?'

'No,' said Brother Tom, very quietly. It was not his place to speak, but he couldn't help it.

'Ah! Listen to your cockroach!' said Père Guillaume. 'Let his wisdom comfort you! Speak, Frère Thomas.'

Peregrine looked up at Brother Tom. 'Yes, you may speak,' he said.

'I cannot presume,' Tom mumbled, self-conscious, 'to tell you what you are. All I can say is that I love you very much. Whatever you may be, it is not in me to love a man who is a proud hypocrite. And I think you should eat your supper.'

Father Peregrine smiled. 'Forgive me. I am behaving like a child. It is indulgent self-preoccupation on my part. Of your goodness, overlook my discourtesy. Your jesting has unsettled me, Guillaume, for you, as well as I, are vowed to holy poverty.'

'Mais oui, *holy* poverty. To renounce all ownership; to say the tunic my back, the sandals on my feet are not mine—that is holy poverty. To own no estate, no gold or silver, to dress in simplicity and say of nothing, "This is mine,"—that is holy poverty. But the warmth of a good fire on a chilly night, the savoury juices of a sucking pig roast in honey, the delight of old, rich, red wine— these are the bounties of God's immense kindliness! Why should we throw them back in his face? Me, I do not like a leaking roof, or the draughty east wind whistling round my hams, or the lifeless frigidity of water at table. Mon Dieu, there must be some pleasure in life! Our flesh cries out for it!'

Peregrine did not reply at once; then, 'I thought we were supposed to crucify the flesh,' he said quietly.

'Ah, mon père, moderation! You ask too much! Your self-imposed penury is not holy poverty. It is like the poverty of the world. It is...'

'Too much like the real thing, you mean?' interjected Peregrine wryly.

'Non, non, ce n'est pas ça... you wallow in it, mon père. That's what it is.'

'Wallow in it?' Peregrine grimaced thoughtfully, pondering the words, I suppose I do. Jesus wallowed in it, did he not? To choose a stable, not a modest mansion; a cattle trough, not a plain, respectable crib; a cross, not a clean, unexceptional death-bed. How do you judge that? Was it an ostentatious waste of his glory? Does it matter? He said, 'Follow me' and that I mean to do. Our life here is not the poverty of the cross. We do not pretend to it. We are not naked, we are not thirsty, we do not bleed, but we try at least to find the poor carpenter of Nazareth in all that we do—whatever the folly. You think it an unreasonable bargain to lay aside earth's pleasures to win heaven? But he laid aside heaven to win the sons of earth.'

Guillaume leaned back in his chair regarding Peregrine with amusement. 'You have not changed, mon ami. Your rhetoric is as impressive as ever. But you are wrong in one thing. You are too late to win grace, or heaven, or strike any kind of bargain with God. It is not a prize to be won, or a deal to be negotiated. It is a gift, already given. Tu comprends? A gift. Receive it and be glad. Celebrate a little now and then.'

'I ought not to have said we win heaven. It is, as you say, a gift. The free grace of God, the treasure of his love, precious beyond words, it is pure gift. We do know celebration here, Guillaume. I have seen men's faces alight with peace, with joy, content. Good, wholesome food, and enough of it, we have that. All right, it's a bit chilly, I grant you, and we are frugal, but we do not go without.

But the dainties of the rich, platters of silver, and fine linen; in the church, altar frontals of cloth of gold, a chalice studded with jewels—such things would shame our vows.'

'Your purity condemns my self-indulgence. You make me blush, mon père!'

'Guillaume, it's not funny. Why do you mock our simplicity? Am I pretentious to insist on it? No, no it cannot be right to live like kings when we are supposed to be like Jesus. Can it?'

'Ah, my very dear friend, it is because you are a little crazy that I love you so. Le Seigneur, yes, he laid aside everything, and became poverty for us. But we are not Jesus. You over-reach yourself. Be realistic. We—'

'*Are* we not?' Peregrine leaned forward, his eyes burning, urgent in his intent face. 'If we who are the body of Christ are not Jesus, who will ever be? The world has need of the presence of Jesus, in the word of the gospels, in the holy bread and wine and in us. Somewhere in all the cynicisms and disappointments that bind and stunt their lives, men need to find a living Jesus, one who can hear their pain and understand their grief and shame; someone to be the love of God *with* them. It has to be a poor man... doesn't it? To touch and heal the pain of men's poverty? I mean all kinds of poverty: the poverty of their need and their brokenheartedness, of their sin... . It would need a man poor in spirit and poor in means to comfort the loneliness of the poor. It is not possible for a rich man's hand to dry the tears of the poor—is it?'

'How should I reply? I admire you. In a way, you are right, mon frère... but... who can live like this? It is not sensible. What would you have me do with my altar frontals? Give them to a peasant who is short of a blanket? What shall I do with my chalices? Distribute them to beggars, that they may fill them at the horses' trough? And what shall I tell my bishop, my patrons, mes frères?' He leaned forward and spoke with a frown of vehemence, serious enough now: 'The poor carpenter of Nazareth, he would not stand a *chance* in the grand machinery of the church, mon ami. We also have a stable on our estate. He would be at home there.' He looked at Father Peregrine, shaking his head, as he relaxed back into his chair. He speared a small piece of cheese with the point of his knife, and as he put it in his mouth and ate it, he looked thoughtfully at Brother Tom.

'What do you say to all this, Frère Thomas?'

Brother Tom had been sitting patiently, wondering if this involved discussion would never end and marvelling that his abbot could become so engrossed in thought as to become indifferent to a plateful of good food. He looked up at the mention of his name.

'What do I say?' he echoed uncertainly.

'Mais oui. To follow Jesus, must a man live stripped of everything as your abbot would have me believe, or can he without sin enjoy the good things of life if his heart is thankful?'

'Jesus…' Brother Tom struggled for an intelligent answer. 'Well, who is your Jesus? I can see Father Abbot's Jesus in the gospels, but who—where is yours?'

There was a silence, broken by Abbé Guillaume's bellow of laughter and his fist crashing down onto the table.

'Mater Dei! You two together—you are *dangerous* for the gospel! You have caught me in my own folly as you caught that filthy Augustinian, you young rogue! Ahhh, you have finished me! Pour me some more wine, mon frère. Let me drink to your answer.

'Eh bien, enough! Let us turn our talk to other things or you will have me kneeling in tears, promising to distribute the substance of my house to all the vagabonds of France. I know you of old. You will lead me out of prudence into your own wild extremism.

'There is a book in your library, mon père, a valuable book. Our library is impoverished for lack of it. Will you lend it—see, I do not ask you to give, though you are rich and I am poor, in the matter of this little book—only lend it, that my scribes may copy it?'

'What book?'

'Aha! Is this the man upon whom earthly things have no hold? Why do you enquire "What book?", mon ami? What is that to you, who have left all to follow Jésus, the *real* Jésus of the gospels, not the vain idol worshipped by worldly men like me!'

'I didn't say you worshipped a vain idol, nor yet that I am free of worldliness, though I wish to God I were. What book?'

'But a little book, though valuable to me. A little text of Aelred de Rievaulx, a book of sermons I have not seen before. You know the book I mean. I see you do by the possessive glint in your eye!'

'You want to borrow that book of homilies by Abbot Aelred, written and bound by his own hand?'

'Oui.'

'For how long?'

'How long? Since it must be only the spiritual substance of the text you value, and not the book itself, I would have thought you could preach your own homilies the equal of Abbot Aelred's, mon frère. It is a book, only a book. Maybe you will let me keep the original. I can have a very nice copy made for you. Our Frère Jean has an excellent hand...'

'Stop it, Guillaume! How long do you want it for?'

'Three months.'

Peregrine hesitated.

'Oh! Regards, Frère Thomas! Quelle avarice!'

'Oh, very well. You can borrow it. I know you will take care of it. Three months only, though. I will hold you to it.'

'Three months. I will return it myself, guarded in my bosom as though my life depended on it.

'Is that your Compline bell already? Mon père, I am sure that bell has a little crack in it somewhere. It sounds like a bucket...'

'*Guillaume*! No man would find silence a hardship if he had you to live with. 'Twould be sweet refuge from the endless abuse. Come then to prayers.'

The Abbé Guillaume held the door open with all courtesy for

160

Abbot Peregrine to pass through, and winked at Brother Tom as they followed him out into the cloister.

✠   ✠   ✠

In the autumn of that year, as the evenings were drawing in, and the nights were beginning to tingle with the threat of frost though the afternoons still basked in gold, Brother Tom came one afternoon to Father Peregrine's house with a package that Brother Martin, the porter, had asked him to deliver.

'Who has brought this? This is from Père Guillaume. Stay a minute.' He undid the parcel, which contained the little book of Aelred de Rievaulx's homilies and a letter. Peregrine read through the letter swiftly, and looked up at Tom.

'Do you read French? No? Let me tell you what he says, then. He sends you his greetings. He remembers you with affection; says he has no cockroaches in the whole of his house; he has searched it nostalgically. Enclosed, the book—his apologies for keeping it these six months. He is sure I am not surprised. (No, I'm not. I'm surprised to get it back this soon.) He would have brought it himself, but his circumstances have changed. He could not forget our conversation here, and when he went back he proposed the sale of all the treasure of his abbey. All of it! Oh Guillaume, bless you, you never did anything by halves. They laughed him to scorn, he says. He resigned himself to accepting their rejection of his proposal, tried to forget the whole thing, but could not. He's made an enemy of his prior and upset the bishop. Dear heaven, that was rash. He has left his community, and gone to live with the Carthusians at St Michel. He says their library is second to none, especially now it has a copy of Abbot Aelred's sermons in it, and he has his own little garden with bees and vegetables. He is rearing a little pig—his mouth waters every time he looks on it. It is good wine country, he says, but not the best, which he laments. He has made some friends among the peasants there, who bring him cheeses and olive oil. How did he manage that, I wonder, in such seclusion? He's bending a rule somewhere if I know him! He has a peach tree in his garden. He says he also has peace in his heart and loves us for what we said. He bids us share a pot of wine by a good fire to remember him, and guard against chilblains in the abominable English cold. The poor carpenter of Nazareth, he says, is teaching him the tricks of his trade. He ends, *Quasi tristes, semper autem gaudentes: sicut egentes, multos autem locupletantes: tamquam nihil habentes et omnia possidentes.* In our sorrows, we always have reason to rejoice: poor ourselves, we bring wealth to many: penniless, we own the world.

'Guillaume de St Michel. Oh Tom, I hope he's done the right thing.'

'What do you mean?'

'Well, he's given up all he had—status, comfort, wealth. The Carthusian Rule is very austere.'

'And he has exchanged it for peace in his heart. I thought that was the bargain you urged him to make.'

'It was. Yes, it was. What looks like sacrifice is the richest treasure of all. I know it, I know. I have chosen Jesus to be my heaven, and him in all his poverty, all his grief. It's just that sometimes I get cold feet.'

✠ ✠ ✠

In the quiet bedroom, I listened to my sisters breathing and the wind blowing round the roof of the house outside.

Mother leaned down and picked up the tall candlestick from the floor.

'They're asleep,' she whispered. 'Shall we go downstairs?' I nodded. We tiptoed out of the room and went quietly down the stairs. As I opened the door of the living room, and the lamplight shone out into the passage, Mother blew out the candle.

CHAPTER EIGHT

The Road Climbs Upwards

Father Carnforth, the retired priest who acted as curate in our parish, had come to tea. He sat in the middle of our sofa, by the fire, Mary on one side and Beth on the other. Cecily had already greeted him, and her conversation with him had been, as usual, brief, factual and to the point: 'Have you got any pepppermints today?'

Father Carnforth smiled at her, and laughed his wheezy laugh. Beth liked to watch his face when he smiled. 'A thousand, thousand smile wrinkles,' she said to Mother, 'are hidden in his face. Then he smiles and you can see them all.'

Father Carnforth had no objections to Cecily's straightforward method of approach. Mother said he was one of the few adults who could have a conversation with Cecily without Mother having to stand there saying, 'Hush, Cecily. Don't be rude, Cecily,' every five seconds like a parrot.

'I have a new bag of peppermints in my pocket, as a matter of fact,' he said. 'I had an idea when I woke up this morning that today I might be needing some. So I went to Mrs Sykes' shop and I said, "Mrs Sykes, I need half a pound of peppermints. Not a quarter today, Mrs Sykes. Half a pound. If you please." Why do you ask? Would you like one?'

'Two,' said Cecily.

'Here you are, then. Two, and one for luck.'

There are some grown-ups who offer you sweets and you'd love one, but somehow all by itself you hear your voice saying, 'Oh, not for me, thank you.' Father Carnforth was not one of them. We were soon all sucking peppermints happily, watching the fire blaze up.

'Ah, I do like a log fire, my dear,' he said to Mother. 'My housekeeper will only buy coal, I regret to say. She says it burns hotter, which is true of course, but what evil, sulphurous smoke it has. This is like incense by comparison.'

Mother had baked scones for tea, which we had with strawberry jam and cream cheese, and she had made an enormous fruit cake and some coffee meringues. We ate everything, the whole fruitcake even. Nobody spoke much while we were eating except to say things like, 'Yes please,' and, 'Pass the butter.'

Afterwards, Father Carnforth wiped his mouth with his napkin and sighed contentedly. 'I think I could just manage one more cup of tea, my dear,' he said. 'Would it offend you if I were to light my pipe?'

Father Carnforth smoked a lovely fragrant blend of pipe tobacco. Mother said she had sometimes been tempted to follow him up the road just to go on sniffing it.

'My doctor says I should give this up,' said Father Carnforth as he held the match flame to the tobacco and drew at his pipe. 'He says my wheezy chest is all down to smoking. I expect he's right. "You're going downhill this year, James," he says to me, but I *am* eighty-three. What can you expect? "If you mean my chest is worse," I said to him, "I will accept your judgement as a medical man, but don't tell me I'm going downhill. The road climbs upwards, upwards to the light. It must do. It wouldn't be such hard going if it was going downhill." You have to be positive about this life, my dear; you know that. Bother, it's gone out already. Pass me my matches, Mary, my sweet. That's it. My dear wife, God rest her soul, used to tell me this was the filthiest, most time-consuming way of wasting money she could possibly think of. She was right, of course; she was right. But there we are; it has given me a lot of pleasure. Good food and good conversation, and a pipe by the fire: what better riches could life have to offer? What's that Cecily? Still room in your tummy for one more peppermint? Here you are, then. One more, and one for luck.'

Mary snuggled up closer to Father Carnforth. He was the oldest person she knew and she was always afraid he was going to die. She often asked him about it. He put his arm around her now, and looked down at her, smiling a kindly reassurance.

'What have they taught you at school this week, little Mary?'

'We are doing a project on dinosaurs. Mrs Kirkpatrick has been telling us what the world was like in prehistoric days.'

Father Carnforth laughed so much he began to cough.

'Dear me, dear me,' he wheezed. 'That must be useful to you. And how does Mrs Kirkpatrick know what the world was like before history began?'

Mary looked nonplussed. 'She does know. She tells us all about it. About the dinosaurs, what they did and what they looked like, and how people used to have tails and lots of hair.'

Father Carnforth looked at the dark grey hair growing on the back of his hand. There was a lot of it.

'Ah, yes,' he said. 'Some of us have progressed less than others, I suppose. I daresay it is a sign of the times that people teach little children with confidence and authority what they cannot possibly know anything about, and have nothing to tell them about the true meaning and development of life. Don't you think, my dear?'

Mother nodded. 'A lot of what they teach them now is above their heads. Mary came down on Tuesday morning saying she would like some vitamins for breakfast. We live in an age of intellectual sophistication and spiritual darkness, I'm afraid. Mind you, I'm glad I don't have to teach them. The spiritual darkness is more in evidence in the classroom than the intellectual sophistication from all I hear.'

Daddy leaned forward and picked up the poker to prod the fire. 'I like Mrs Kirkpatrick,' he said. 'She has more about her than some. Beware of toppling her from her pedestal. Little ones respect their teachers enormously, and it's right they should.'

'Respect is fine, but not mindless acceptance,' said Mother, 'however young they are.'

'Have no fear, my dear. Your children are nothing if not strong-minded. Isn't that so, Cecily? Well now, it's my turn to say Evensong, so I must tear myself away from your fireside. Pull me to my feet, Beth and Mary. Thank you. Thank you so much, my dears. I have enjoyed myself immensely. I expect I shall see you all on Sunday.'

Daddy helped him into his coat, and stood with Mother at our door, watching him walk up the hill towards the parish church.

'We shall miss him sorely when the time comes,' said Mother as she closed the door and came back into the living room to curl up on the sofa by the fire. 'Father Bennett's all right if you can stand it, but I do love that old man.'

She sat there, watching the fire, while Daddy and Beth cleared away the tea things. Mary went with them to help wash up, and Therese got into the bath. She was going out in the evening, to the cinema, and wanted to wash her hair. The lovely scent of her bath stuff drifted through the house. Mother sniffed it. 'Mmm. This has been an afternoon of nice smells,' she said. 'Where's Cecily? It's very quiet.'

I went to look. She had fallen asleep playing with her toys upstairs in our bedroom.

'So you could tell me a story, Mother,' I said as I sat down again by the fire. Mother glanced through the window at the overcast sky and drizzling rain. 'It's a story kind of day,' she said, 'not fit for much else.'

'Tell me a story about Father Peregrine with Melissa in it; Melissa and her children.'

'Melissa... she doesn't come into many of the stories, you

know. The monks told the stories to her, so she wasn't part of the stories. But there are one or two times she was there and had her own memories to pass on. Melissa… . Now then, there was one story, yes. Put another log on the fire, my love. Yes, I remember it now.'

✠ ✠ ✠

Melissa had brought her children to the abbey to stay through the last watch of Lent and celebrate the Easter feast. She never saw very much of Father Peregrine when she came at Easter; there were too many other demands on his time. Already the guest house was almost full with visitors and pilgrims who had come to share in the resurrection festival. Still, she liked to be there with him following the long, sorrowful journey of Holy Week, and the explosion of triumph as the tables were turned on death itself on Easter Day.

There was another reason, too, why she came at Easter. It was on Easter Monday eleven years ago that Father Peregrine had been beaten and disfigured, his hands maimed and his leg crippled. It was a time of year when the sharpness of memories pressed painfully upon him, and old terrors stirred. Melissa knew that. She knew that most of the brothers would be rushed off their feet caring for guests and carrying out the rites of the Easter liturgies, on top of the round of work and prayer that was a daily necessity. They would likely be too busy to glimpse the horror and panic that sometimes came very close to the surface in Abbot Peregrine on Easter Day. She had asked him once, straight out, 'How is it for you. Father, at Easter-time? There are some bitter memories there for you.'

He had sat in silence a long while before answering her, and when he did speak, it was hesitantly, reluctantly.

'Holy Week is not too bad. I… Jesus in Gethsemane… I… he… that is the source of all my peace. There have been,

167

there's no point in trying to hide it, times when I've thought I would go under in the fear and helplessness—despair really—that overwhelms me some days. I have held myself together, just, but... the dread of breaking apart before the whole community, I can't tell you. His terror and distress in Gethsemane... you can see his soul writhe... it answers, more profoundly than I could express, the intolerable... how can I explain it? The words go round and round in my head, "I can't bear it, I can't bear it," behind all I am saying or doing, filling all my silences. It steadies me to hear his humbleness, "Lord, if it be possible—take this cup from me." Then I know what courage is, where to find it. Good Friday, and the cross... nails through his hands... oh, God!... Melissa, *nails...*'

Peregrine paused and shook his head, his face contorted at the horror and pain of it.

'Nails through his hands! On Good Friday morning I kneel before the crucifix in my chamber and I stretch out my hands to him, and I say, "Crucified one... beautiful one... Redeemer... Saviour... Lamb of God... you heal us by your wounds. Can you make something of these broken, ugly hands... put them to some use?" But Easter Day—Easter Day is another thing. Christ is risen and I know, I *do* know, that is my salvation. I understand that it is my glory, and my hope. Without his rising, our suffering would embitter us beyond redeeming, I know it. Only... he is in glory, and I am still in Gethsemane. He is in triumph and I am still pinned to my cross. On Easter Day he leaves me behind. Besides all that, it is our busiest time, and I do wonder at times, I confess it, if one day among the crowd, they will come again and finish their vengeance on my body. For they meant to have my life. I greet the pilgrims, and I must smile at them, and welcome them lovingly as I should. But all the while I am watching, wondering. Well, no, not all the while. I exaggerate. But the old terror is still there. I feel sick with it sometimes. It's hard to control. Don't mistake me, death I do not fear... but pain, infirmity, helplessness.

When I walk through the church and I hear someone behind me, I am cold, sweating, terrified. I have tried to overcome it. God knows, I have prayed. I am ashamed to have so little joy in Christ's most glorious day. It is not for want of trying.'

He sat looking down at his misshapen hands. The craftsmanship and costliness of the abbot's ring decorated the right hand incongruously, its opulence mocking their ugliness. They showed starkly against the unrelieved black of his tunic. Melissa wondered how often in a day he looked down at his hands, and if there was ever a time when he thought nothing of it, being merely accustomed to their brokenness.

He raised his eyes to look at her. Usually his gaze was full of warmth, of love; the heart of his giving, passing on the peace of God. But for once he let her look into him and see just what he was; his sadness, his pain, the frustration that raged in the man trapped inside the living prison of his disabled body.

'It's a poor thing, isn't it, that the abbot of a monastery should be so...' He paused, searching for the word he wanted.

'Human?' she said.

She did not forget the conversation, or his sadness and his sense of shame, and she tried when she could to be there at Easter. When she came, she brought her children too. They were growing fast. The youngest, Benedict, was almost two, and his days were one long disaster of joyful exploration. Nicholas, her oldest child, was just eight years old. In between came Anne, a little more than a year younger than Nicholas but twice his age for wisdom and common sense, and Catherine, who was just four, candid, passionate and therefore a continual source of embarrassment to her parents.

As soon as they arrived at the abbey, the children made for the kitchen and Brother Cormac, who was their hero. They were a little bit afraid of Brother Andrew, the fierce old Scot who was the cook and monarch of the kitchen's self-contained kingdom, but Cormac told them stories and fed them tit-bits, and took them to see the lambs and the calves in his free time. Cormac also knew where the birds and the field mice nested, and won their undying admiration by being able to spit a cherry-stone even further than Nicholas, who had been practising for weeks. It was Cormac who made them a swing and climbed to a dizzy height in a tall elm tree to secure it to a branch. It was Cormac who took them sledging in the winter on the steep hill that sheltered the guest house and played hide-and-seek with them among the straw bales in the barn. He showed them how to call the owls at night so that they would answer, and he played fivestones with them in the summer dust, and they loved him dearly.

'Don't plague the life out of the kitchen brothers, now!' Melissa called after them as they vanished across the abbey court, 'and mind Benedict near the well!' They were not listening. She watched them go, and then turned back to the guest house. She felt happiness bubbling up inside her, a pressure of joy. She loved to be at the abbey. It was a harbour of peace for her, a place to rebuild her strength. There are not many places where a woman with four small children is welcomed with unfeignedly joyful hospitality, but this was one of them.

She stood leaning her back against the rough stone wall of the guest house, looking across the flagged court at the huge abbey church rising like a great rock of strength and assurance. She sighed contentedly and went in at the guest house door. She saw Peregrine before he saw her, limping slowly across the hall. He had come in search of her, having been sent word of her arrival.

'Father! God save you, you look tired to death!'

His face lit in a smile of welcome and he hugged her to him. 'It's good to see you, dear one. Oh, I've been looking forward to this! Have you lost all your babes to the kitchens already? Well then, come and share some of Brother Walafrid's blackberry wine with me, and we've been given some figs that are good. We can have a moment of quiet together. Oh, but forgive me, selfish. Maybe you are too weary after your journey? Would you rather rest first, dear heart?'

Melissa smiled at him, loving him, soaking up the luxury of being cherished, made to feel special. 'It's you I've come to see,' she said happily. 'If you've a spare moment, I'm going to seize it before someone else does. I can rest later.'

✠ ✠ ✠

The children found Brother Cormac finishing the preparations for the cold evening meal that the community would eat after Vespers. He was pleased to see them, but he looked slightly harassed.

'Oh, ho! Ho! It's you, you demons! Search in the store, little Annie, and you'll find apples and honey—you know where the bread is. If you'll take some out to the cloister to nibble, I'll come presently and take you to see the new foal and the bats in the church tower. I mustn't come for another few minutes yet though. Brother Andrew's turned into a dragon today and he'll scorch me with his fiery breath if I stop working for one moment. Find yourselves something to eat and skedaddle, there's good children. I'll come out to you when I can.' And with these words he disappeared into the dairy to fetch the pitcher of milk from its cool stone shelf.

Catherine moved closer to her sister. 'Has Brother Andrew really turned into a dragon?' It did not seem unlikely.

'No, stupid. Cormac just means he's in a bad temper,' said Nicholas scornfully. 'Come on, let's get some bread and honey and apples before he comes.'

They sat out in the cloister which gave a fair shelter from the chill March wind, and ate the things they had found. Benedict transferred most of his honey, generously ladled out by Nicholas, from his bread to his hair and clothes, and then turned his attention to rooting up the flowers that were Brother Fidelis' pride and joy.

171

'Glory be to God!' gasped Cormac as he finally emerged from the kitchen and caught sight of Benedict. 'Is that a child or a compost heap? Let me give you a scrub, for mercy's sake or your mother will be scolding me, and I've been scolded enough already for one day.'

He seized Benedict and holding him well away from himself, he carried him through the kitchen to the yard at the back, and set him down on the cobbles beside the well, ignoring the little child's indignant yells of protest. The other children trooped through behind him. 'Fetch me a towel, Annie,' said Cormac. 'You'll find some back in the cloister, in the lavatorium, next to the refectory. Nicholas, a bucket of water if you will. Thank you. That will do nicely. Now then.' He kept a firm grip on Benedict as he spoke, and stripped his clothes from him and sluiced him thoroughly under the icy water. Not brought up to monastic asceticism, Benedict roared with pain and rage when he could get his breath back. Brother Cormac took not the slightest bit of notice, but briskly rubbed the little body with the towel Anne had found until Benedict was pink and glowing; then wrapped him up in it and proceeded to rinse his clothes.

'Stop screaming, child. Think you a worm or a mole that you can go burrowing in the earth and come up clean? Come now, that's the worst of it off. Let's go and rummage in your bags in the guest house and see if we can find some clean clothing before your mother sees you. Here, I'll carry you. Nicholas, bring his clothes. We'll set them to dry before the fire. I've wrung them well, but they may drip still, so mind you hold them away from you and don't get yourself all wet. That's it.'

Cormac took them as he promised up into the bell tower of the abbey church and showed them the bats hanging in the dimness, and to the stable to see the spotted foal, very young, bedded with her mother in clean straw. They collected the eggs from the henhouses, and carried them back to the kitchen, brown and snow white and speckled, and one of a pale, rosy beige, which Cormac said was laid by Dame Cluck, the sovereign of the poultry yard and the cockerel's favourite wife. He took them into the warming room to say hello to the two or three brothers there who had come down from the scriptorium to warm fingers that were numb with cold at the great fireplace. Just before Vespers he returned them to their mother, and she thanked him warmly.

'Brother Cormac, you're an angel! Many, many thanks. Look at them: tired and happy. All I need to do is feed them and put them to bed. Oh—what happened to Benedict's clothes?'

Cormac grinned at her. 'An angel, is it? By'r lady, I shall need to be this week. We've that much work in the kitchen it's beyond mortal man. His clothes you will find drying by the fire, not entirely clean, but recognisable now. I'll take the children to see the lambs tomorrow, but not till the afternoon. There's the Vespers bell now, I must be on my way. The thanks are all mine; I've loved their company.'

He kissed Benedict and handed him over into his mother's arms, rested his hands lightly a moment on Anne's and Catherine's heads, nodded to Nicholas as one man to another, and was gone. Melissa took them to eat their supper in the guest house refectory after they had washed their hands and picked the straw out of their hair and clothes. A bowl of new milk had been set for each of them, and a small loaf of fresh bread, wrapped in a linen cloth. There was a pat of rich, yellow butter on an earthenware plate, some soft, white cheese, salted slightly and delicately flavoured by the herbs that had wrapped it, and a wooden bowl of sweet yellow apples from the store, polished until they glowed in the firelight like lamps.

'Brother Dominic says the abbey is supposed to reflect the peace and order of heaven,' said Melissa to her children as she sat Benedict on her lap and helped him with his milk, 'and it does. I can't think of heaven being much different from this.' She smiled peacefully.

'That's because,' said Nicholas, tearing a large piece of bread off the loaf and spreading it vigorously with plenty of butter, 'you haven't heard Brother Cormac and Brother Andrew arguing in the kitchen.'

Melissa looked at him with a little frown of irritation. 'Nicholas, don't put so much food in your mouth at once,' she said sharply. She did not want her dream shattered. 'I'm sure they don't argue.'

'They do. They're terrible, worse than us. Brother Damian says you could light a candle from the sparks that fly between them. It's because Cormac's cooking's so awful and he doesn't like doing the meat and the fish. Brother Andrew says to him, "What would you like me to do with these rolls, Brother? Will I put them on the table, or are you saving them for a sling-shot? But half of one of these would slay Goliath nicely," and Cormac glares at him from under his eyebrows and mutters. He *swears*. Yes he *does*, Mother, I've heard him.'

'Nicholas, I'm sure you're making all this up. *I've* never heard Brother Cormac swear. Father Abbot says those two love each other like father and son. Now stop talking and eat your supper. Look, Catherine's falling asleep over her food.'

'They may love each other, but it doesn't stop them…'

'Nicholas! Enough. Don't speak with your mouth full either.'

When they had eaten everything in sight and left nothing but a sprinkling of crumbs and a scrape of butter, Melissa shepherded them upstairs and into bed.

'Brother Cormac,' said Catherine sleepily, as Melissa tucked her and Anne into the bed they shared, 'knows what the rabbits think. He knows what the words are of the song the thrush is singing. It is saying, "*Can… cantabo…*" what did he say Annie?'

'*Cantabo Domino in vita mea*,' Anne recited carefully. 'But I don't know what it means.'

'I will sing to the Lord as long as I live,' said Melissa softly. 'Is that what Brother Cormac says the thrush is singing?'

She told Father Peregrine about it as they sat together over their evening meal, and he smiled.

'Brother Cormac, yes, it wouldn't surprise me at all if he understood the song of the birds. He loves the wild creatures. He used at one time to love birds and beasts more than he loved mankind. It distresses him to see anything wounded and killed. He likes them to be free. I've seen him in the kitchen preparing a fowl for the pot. Brother Andrew will be standing there with the bird dangling by its feet, neglected in his hand, as he issues orders or corrects someone's work, and he'll dump it on Brother Cormac—"Pluck this and gut it please, Brother." Brother Cormac will take it into his hands with its poor dead head supported on his wrist, and carry it to the workbench so, and lay it down reverently, and strip it of its feathers as tenderly and gently as a woman laying a sleepy babe to rest. It irritates Brother Andrew no end. Ah, no doubt about it, the kitchen work is a hard discipline for Brother Cormac sometimes.'

'Couldn't he do something else—work in the garden or something instead?'

'Yes, he could—now he could. There were reasons for keeping him to the kitchen at one time. He helps in the infirmary and he helps Brother Mark with his bees, but he likes to work with Brother Andrew. They have a good understanding. Brother Cormac had no family of his own, and Brother Andrew has come to be like a father to him; answered a need in him somehow. There was no love lost between them in the early days, though. Two of a kind, they are. A bit too much alike for comfort sometimes.'

'Brother Cormac's good to my children. He took them to see the bats in the church tower today, and he says he'll take them to see the young lambs tomorrow when he can escape from the kitchen in the afternoon.'

'Maundy Thursday, yes, the brothers are fasting before the evening Mass. He'll maybe find some free time. He needs some. He's been carrying most of Brother Andrew's work lately. Brother Andrew is feeling his age. He's been tired, very tired and a bit breathless of late. He has a look sometimes as though he's in pain, but he'll not admit to it. Brother Cormac has been doing all he can to spare him in the kitchen.'

'Oh, then...' Melissa looked concerned. 'Should he be spending this time with my children? I don't want them to be a burden.'

'No, no.' Peregrine shook his head. 'Brother Cormac delights in your children. They have extra help in the kitchen during the Easter feast. Brother Damian is there, and Brother Mark. Let it be.'

✠ ✠ ✠

In the morning, when her children went out to play, Melissa cautioned them, 'Don't go bothering Brother Cormac, now. This afternoon, he said. You must wait until then. Go for a walk down to the infirmary and say hello to Uncle Edward.'

But Catherine stole away, and appeared at Cormac's side in the kitchen, where she stood in solemn silence as she watched him gutting fish for the midday meal.

'Is that a fish?' she asked at last.

'It is,' he replied shortly. He hated the job and it put him out of sorts to do it. He cut the head away deftly with the sharp knife, and slit the belly, flicking out the spilling mess of guts with the knife point.

'Oh, Cormac,' said Catherine in a shocked voice, 'you've cut off its face.'

Cormac closed his eyes and swallowed hard. He felt distinctly queasy. 'Catherine!' Anne's voice called from the doorway. 'Catherine! Mother says you're not to bother Cormac in the morning. You've got to stay with us.'

'But Cormac is cutting the fishes' tummies open and throwing their insides away,' protested Catherine. 'I want to stay and watch.'

Cormac put down the knife and wiped his hands. He picked Catherine up and carried her to the door. He deposited her firmly outside.

'You do as your mother says,' he said, and closed the door behind her.

'You didn't do anything naughty, did you, Catherine?' asked Anne, anxiously. 'He looked a bit cross.' But Catherine was already running along the cloister, heading for the infirmary.

Brother Cormac returned grimly to his task, stuffed the fish carcasses with herbs and butter and left them packed in neat lines in a covered dish ready to be baked.

Brother Andrew called him from the other side of the room: 'Brother Cormac! It's time you did those fish. You've not got all the morning.' He sounded tired and irritable.

'But I...' began Cormac.

'"But" nothing, Brother. There's bread to be baked for tomorrow and they need a hand in the guest house kitchen, so will you set about it and get them done.'

'But, Brother...'

'Brother Cormac, it *needs doing*!' Andrew shouted at him. Cormac's black brows were gathering in a frown and his blue eyes were as cold as frost.

'Come *on*, Brother Cormac!' roared Andrew.

'I have done the fish,' Cormac said from between clenched teeth with slow and deliberate fury, glowering at the old man.

Brother Andrew clicked his tongue in exasperation. 'Then why the devil didn't you say so?' he snapped.

Cormac looked as though he was about to boil over. The kitchen staff kept their heads bent to their work. Neither Brother Andrew nor Brother Cormac was the most patient of men, and minor confrontations were a common occurrence. For a moment the two of them glared at each other, then, 'Whatever *ails* you today?' said Cormac more gently. 'You're like a bear with a sore head. I've done the fish. Shall I make a start on the bread or go over to the guest house?'

'I—*oh*!' Brother Andrew clutched at the table where he stood, gasping with sudden pain. The colour drained from his face and beads of sweat stood out on his brow.

Cormac was across the room to him in an instant and Brother Andrew turned to him and gripped his arms convulsively, bent over in pain.

'Get Brother John,' said Cormac to Brother Damian, who left at a run. 'Where does it hurt you?' he asked Brother Andrew, looking anxiously at the old man's face as he tried to stand erect. It was deathly pale, the lips blue and set in a tight line of pain.

'It—*ah*!' Andrew gasped and clung to him. 'Like a great hand squeezing my ribs. Like... bands of iron. *Ah*! It's not been this bad before.'

'Lie down,' said Cormac. 'Here, on the floor. Come, rest your head on my lap, so. There now. Brother John will be with us from the infirmary.' The old man could not keep still, but writhed in his pain. His hand gripped Cormac's knee fiercely, and he pressed his face into his thigh. Brother Cormac could feel the agonised contortion of it, and the old man's trembling passed through into his own body. Oh John, hurry, he thought, desperately. Oh Jesu, mercy.

Brother Andrew drew up his knees in pain and groaned. Sweat was pouring from him. Brother Mark bent over them offering a cold, damp cloth. Cormac took it without looking up, and tenderly wiped the old man's head and neck and as much of his face as he could get to.

Brother John came hurrying through the door and knelt beside them. 'All right, we'll carry him to the infirmary. Two of you men here, make a chair for him with your hands. We'll carry him so.'

'I'll come with you,' said Cormac.

'You... will... not...' gasped Brother Andrew, fighting for breath. 'You'll get... the meal... to the table—and Brother— don't... burn... the bread.' Then he screwed up his eyes and clamped his mouth shut as another wave of pain engulfed him. He looked very old and shrunken and frail as they carried him out of the door. Brother Cormac watched them go, his face almost as white as Andrew's, but as the door closed behind them, he turned resolutely to his work.

'Put the fish in to bake, Brother Damian. John, fill the pitchers with ale. Water it, but not so much as yesterday; they were grumbling. Brother Mark, take the bread from its proving and knead it again. Luke, Simon, go down to the guest house and see what you can do.'

He himself continued the preparation of a green salad that Brother Andrew had begun, his face taut with anxiety, his hands trembling. Brother Damian came up quietly behind him and put an arm around his shoulders. Cormac shook him off irritably.

'Come *on*, Brother. Have you done that fish? Good. Watch the pot of beans on the fire. They're nearly done. They mustn't overcook or they'll go to a mush. Drat, there's the Office bell. You go, both of you. I can finish off here. Is the bread ready for its second proving? Thank you. Cover it with a cloth before you go. No, set it to rise there, near the fire. Yes, yes. Go now, then.'

When the Office was over, Cormac listened to the soft slapping of the brothers' sandalled feet coming along the cloister, and the indefinable whisper of their robes as they passed the open door, the splash of water in the lavatorium as they washed their hands. Oh, hurry, he pleaded silently, please hurry. But they filtered through into the refectory with their usual dignified calm.

Brother Cormac made the kitchen tidy, and saw the meal to the table. He did not join the brethren to eat, but restlessly paced the kitchen floor, listening to the drone of the reader's voice and the subdued background sound of the meal: pottery on wood, metal on pot. Then pot on pot and metal on metal as the servers stacked the bowls and collected the spoons and knives. Cormac served the kitcheners, the reader and the servers with their meal as they came through into the kitchen from the refectory, and then he left them to it and ran to the infirmary. In the ante-room he found Father Peregrine sitting with Catherine playing at his feet. Anne sat beside him, very quiet, her eyes gravely fixed on Brother Cormac as he hastened through the door and stopped, looking helplessly to Father Peregrine for reassurance.

'Is he——?'

'They could not save him,' said Peregrine gently. 'He was gone by the time they got him to bed.'

'No...' whispered Cormac. 'For God's sake, *no*. Where is he?'

'Just through there.' Father Peregrine watched him stumble through the door. The room Cormac entered was airy and chill, filled with the cold light of spring. It was utterly silent except for the faint squeaking and tapping of leaves outside crowding against one of the windows. There was no one there but the motionless form on the bed, laid out straight in his habit and sandals. His hair was combed, and his rosary placed among the fingers of his hands folded on his breast. Cormac looked at Brother Andrew's body, white and frozen in the absolute stillness of death; at the toes like carvings and the sculpted silence of his hands, his jaw, his nose. He stood by the bed in the pale spring light and looked down at the deserted house, empty dwelling, that had been his friend. He lifted his hand and caressed the cold forehead and bony cheek.

'We served the meal on time,' he whispered. He took one last long look, stooped and pressed his warm lips to the cold, still brow, his eyes closed. Then he turned away and left the room and closed the door behind him.

'Come and sit down.' Father Peregrine's voice penetrated the daze of shock, and Cormac sat on the bench beside him, his elbows resting on his knees, his hands clasped together, seeing nothing.

'I wish I'd been with him,' he said at last, tonelessly.

Catherine looked up from her game on the floor. 'Cormac, why are you crying?' she asked curiously. 'Is it because of Brother Andrew?'

'I'm not crying,' said Cormac dully, without looking at her.

'Shush, Catherine,' said Anne, but Catherine was not to be

180

put off. 'You are,' she insisted. 'Your nose is running and your eyes are full of tears, like Nicholas' when he's trying not to cry. There's a tear running down your face now. I can see it.'

Peregrine stretched out his hand and laid it on Cormac's hands which gripped together till the knuckles were white. Cormac groaned and his head went down on the abbot's hand. Anne darted to his side and spread herself over his shoulders like a bird. Catherine got to her feet and crept close to Peregrine, frightened by the sight of adult grief. 'Is Cormac's heart breaking?' she asked in an awed voice.

Peregrine nodded. 'Yes, Catherine,' he said quietly, 'his heart is breaking. It will take a long time to heal. Go and find your mother now, children. Tell her what has happened. There, Annie, your love has done him good, but let him be now. Go and find Mother.'

✠ ✠ ✠

They buried Brother Andrew's body on Easter Eve in the morning, pushing the bier slowly up the winding path under the dripping beech trees to the brothers' burial ground in the wood; a sober and silent procession of cowled black figures shrouded in the grey morning mist. At the graveside, Cormac stood and watched as they shovelled in the wet earth, his face pale and remote in the shadow of his cowl.

He went about the duties of the day in silence. The kitchen was enclosed in a pall of silence. The absence of Brother Andrew's sarcastic Scots rasp was as vivid among the men there as if they could hear him still.

At midnight the brethren gathered in the choir for the Easter vigil; the moment of solemn joy and mystery when death is turned back, and the victory of the grave disintegrates in its own ashes, for Christ, Morning Star, is risen. The massive church was filled with pilgrims, the rustling dark alive with the excitement of their expectation. The Easter fire was set alight in the darkness, and the

Paschal candle lit from it, the light illuminating the watch of the night, the ranks of brothers in the choir, the crowd of men and women and children in the nave.

Silent and numb, Cormac stood in his stall, grief welling up in him until he could no longer contain it. Tears ran unchecked down his cheeks as he stood watching Father Chad help Father Peregrine to take the great Paschal candle into his scarred and twisted hands. Father Chad stepped back and the abbot lifted up the candle.

'*Lumen Christi*,' his firm voice sang out the triumphant chant, and '*Deo gratias*!' came the thunder of response from all around the church. The light of Christ: thanks be to God. There was, obscurely, hope in the candle held aloft in those maimed hands, the light of Christ.

Is this your healing? Cormac prayed silently in the bitterness of his soul. To waken my heart to love and friendship and then flood it with this pain? Is this your light, your gift, your way—this agony?

He did not expect an answer. He was filled with the anger and desolation of his loss. He was unprepared for the word, whispered deep in his soul, from somewhere as far outside himself as the stars, yet as near as his own shuddering breath: 'Yes.'

Glossary of Terms

Breviary – monastic prayer book

Carthusians – contemplative order; silent hermits in community

Cellarer – monk responsible for oversight of all provisions; a key role in the community

Chapter – daily meeting governing practical matters, where a chapter of St Benedict's Rule was read and expounded by the abbot

Chapter House – meeting room for community affairs

Choir – the part of the church where the community sits

Cloister – covered way giving access to main buildings of monastery

Cistercian – order of monks, reform of Benedictine tradition

Crimplene – an easy-care synthetic fabric

Dorter – dormitory

Esquire – personal assistant to a man of high status

Eucharist – the holy communion meal, the Lord's Supper

Hours – (as in a Book of Hours) the services of worship in the monastic day

Lay – not ordained

Liturgy – structured worship

Office – the set worship taking place at regular intervals through the day

Parlour – small room where conversation was allowed

Physic garden – the medicinal herb patch beside the infirmary

Porter – doorkeeper

Postulant – new member not yet made a novice

Precentor – worship facilitator

Prior – in an abbey, the deputy leader; in a priory, the leader

Rule – the Benedictine Rule: document guiding daily life, written by St Benedict

Monastic Day

There may be slight variations from place to place and at different times from the Dark Ages through the Middle Ages and onward – e.g. Vespers may be after supper rather than before. This gives a rough outline. Slight liberties are taken in my novels to allow human interactions to play out.

Winter Schedule (from Michaelmas)
2:30am Preparation for the nocturns of matins – psalms etc.
3:00am Matins, with prayers for the royal family and for the dead
5:00am Reading in preparation for
6:00am Lauds at daybreak and Prime; wash and break fast (just
          bread and water, standing)
8.30am Terce, Morrow Mass, Chapter
12:00 noon Sext, Sung Mass, midday meal
2.00pm None
4:15pm Vespers, Supper, Collatio
6:15pm Compline
The Grand Silence begins

Summer Schedule
1:30am Preparation for the nocturns of matins – psalms etc.
2:00am Matins
3:30am Lauds at daybreak, wash and break fast
6:00am Prime, Morrow Mass, Chapter
8:00am Terce, Sung Mass
11:30am Sext, midday meal
2:30pm None
5:30pm Vespers, Supper, Collatio
8:00pm Compline
The Grand Silence begins

Liturgical Calendar

I have included the main feasts and fasts in the cycle of the church's year, plus one or two other dates that are mentioned (e.g. Michaelmas and Lady Day when rents were traditionally collected) in these stories.

Advent – begins four Sundays before Christmas

Christmas – December 25th

Holy Innocents – December 28th

Epiphany – January 6th

Baptism of our Lord concludes Christmastide, Sunday after January 6th

Candlemas – February 2 (Purification of Blessed Virgin Mary, Presentation of Christ in the temple)

Lent – Ash Wednesday to Holy Thursday – start date varies with phases of moon

Holy Week – last week of Lent and the Easter Triduum

Lady Day – March 25th

Easter Triduum (three days) of Good Friday, Holy Saturday, Easter Sunday

Ascension – forty days after Easter

Whitsun (Pentecost) – fifty days after Easter

Trinity Sunday – Sunday after Pentecost

Corpus Christi – Thursday after Trinity

Sacred Heart of Jesus – Friday of the following week

Feast of John the Baptist – June 24th

Lammas (literally 'loaf-mass'; grain harvest) – August 1st

Michaelmas – feast of St Michael and All Angels, September 29th

All Saints – November 1st

All Souls – November 2nd

Martinmas – November 11th